"I found this in the master bedroom in the main house," Tyler said.

Gracie reached for it and then pulled her hand back. "What is it?"

"A bug. And it means whoever is listening is close."

"There was someone in my father's house, who planted those things?" Her usual calm deserted her. A burning resentment was starting to grow in her belly. "Did you find any in the pool house?"

"Not yet."

She clenched her fist around the tiny device. "I can't believe this. Why would someone bug my house?"

He slid his big, warm hand under her fist and, one by one, peeled back her cold fingers until the bug dropped into his hand.

"I'll take care of this, Gracie. If you let me."

As he turned to walk away, he brushed his fingers across her knuckles. Just that.

Her breath hitched. She had to make herself take another one.

Houses rigged to blow up, bugs and six-foot-something of ex-DEA danger.

She was in so much trouble.

Books by Stephanie Newton

Love Inspired Suspense

*Perfect Target
*Moving Target
*Smoke Screen
*Flashpoint
*Holiday Havoc
  "Christmas Target"
*Point Blank Protector

*Emerald Coast 911

STEPHANIE NEWTON

penned her first suspense story—complete with illustrations—at the age of twelve, but didn't write seriously until her youngest child was in first grade. She lives in northwest Florida, where she gains inspiration from the sugar-white sand, aqua-blue-green water of the Gulf of Mexico, and the many unusual and interesting things you see when you live on the beach. You can find her most often enjoying the water with her family, or at their church, where her husband is the pastor. Visit Stephanie at her website, www.stephanienewton.net or send an email to newtonwriter@gmail.com.

POINT BLANK PROTECTOR

STEPHANIE NEWTON

Love Inspired

Recycling programs
for this product may
not exist in your area.

LOVE INSPIRED BOOKS

ISBN-13: 978-0-373-67459-6

POINT BLANK PROTECTOR

www.LoveInspiredBooks.com

Printed in U.S.A.

Let us then approach the throne of grace
with confidence, so that we may receive mercy
and find grace to help us in our time of need.
— *Hebrews* 4:16

For my daughter, courageous in spirit

Acknowledgments:

My heartfelt thanks to my editor at Steeple Hill, Melissa Endlich, and my agent, Melissa Jeglinski. I'm blessed to work with a dream team of extremely talented people!

Thanks to my friends and critique partners Brenda Minton and Holly LaPat—I'm so glad to know that I don't have to make this journey alone.

Many, many thanks to writer friend Elise Parker who managed to keep me awake and motivated during late-night writing sessions. Dude!

Thanks also to Brian Stampfl of CSI Seattle, who has seen many a crime scene and always seems to have a good idea when I need one. He also writes a very funny blog at www.csiseattle.blogspot.com.

Finally, thanks to Sara and Kate from Our Best Bites, who gave Tyler the recipe for Cheese Biscuits and gave me the idea for the manly blowtorch for the crème brûlée. You can find these recipes and more at www.ourbestbites.com.

ONE

Tyler Clark hated seeing the shrink. Hated having his motives questioned, his mind probed. He pulled open the door to the Sea Breeze Police Department and showed his ID.

The watch officer took one brief look at Tyler's face and slid the visitor's pass across the desk. "Have a nice day."

Tyler resented jumping through hoops for bureaucratic nonsense, and he really couldn't stand being jerked out of the field until the crazy task had been completed. Crazy because any undercover agent worth his salt could fool a shrink.

But regular evals were part of his job as an undercover agent—at least, they had been part of his job until he'd been exposed by the press after his last case closed. As a bonus, his new job—*interim* job, he reminded himself—also required a visit to the shrink. Lucky him.

In his experience, shrinks came in two varieties, the cheerful and sympathetic wanna-be-your-friend type and the slice-and-dice, cut-out-the-cancer type. He didn't like either one, preferring to deal with things on his own time. Or not.

The utilitarian gray halls of the Sea Breeze, Florida, Police Department weren't complicated, and within minutes of entering the building he found Dr. VanDoren's second-floor office.

The doctor had a white message board on the outside of the door. Someone had drawn a smiley face on it. Great. VanDoren was one of *those*.

He pushed the cracked door all the way open, knocking on it with two knuckles.

The woman at the desk was on the phone. Lake-blue eyes widened as he entered the room. She pulled an appointment book from a teetering pile on her desk and ran a finger down it, still speaking softly into the phone.

When her finger reached his name, she looked up, giving him a bright smile. She motioned to a chair and raised a finger for him to wait.

He eyed the club chairs. In one she'd left her purse and computer bag. In the other a neat stack of papers and assorted files. He picked up the stack and laid it on the corner of her desk.

Tyler relaxed into the soft leather and watched her as she talked on the phone. She'd turned slightly away from him toward the window. As she spoke, her hands moved in animated gestures. Bright April sunlight streamed in, gilding the corkscrew blond curls.

"All right, then. Talk to you later." She placed the phone on its cradle. "What can I do for you?"

"I'm here to see the doctor."

"About?" She picked what looked like a random envelope from a stack of mail and sliced into it with a wicked letter opener sporting the police seal on its handle.

He stared unblinking, waiting while she glanced over the sheet of paper before tossing it into the trash can. When she lifted her eyes to meet his again, he said, "I think I'll just talk to the doctor—"

She raised one slim eyebrow, a private joke sparkling in her eyes.

Right. "You're Dr. VanDoren."

"Yep." The doc picked up another envelope and cut it open, giving the contents a cursory glance before it followed the last one into the trash can.

"I bet you're killer on the witness stand." He didn't stop to think that his words weren't exactly complimentary.

The psychologist tilted her head. "Defense attorneys do tend to underestimate me."

Another envelope lost its fight with the slick blade in her hand. This one she filed on top of a lopsided pile on her desk before she met his eyes again with a faintly perplexed look, as if surprised to find he was still sitting there. "So why are you here, Mr. Clark?"

"Tyler." He forced himself to sit still. He'd done the same thousands of times before when he'd been undercover and under the close scrutiny of everyone from drug lords to mafia kingpins.

The doc laid the letter opener on top of a stack of unopened envelopes and turned her full attention to him. "Tyler, then. What brings you to my office this morning?"

She surely had to have been briefed by Captain Conyers, but the rule with shrinks, if there was one, was to play along. With practiced ease, he relaxed into the moment, showing her the person she wanted to see.

"I've worked undercover for the DEA for the past several years, mostly in Chicago. My cover was blown nationwide during that big bust the SBPD made a few weeks ago. Basically I had two choices. I could work a desk for the DEA or I could go out on my own."

She laced her fingers, leaning forward on her elbows. "So you decided to go out on your own. What brings you back to Sea Breeze?"

"The personal reason—my family is here. Professionally, I know how drug dealers think. I'm here to teach certain techniques to your police force so that they can spot an infiltration into your community before it gets out of control."

"Your consulting job isn't what brought you to my office." Doc VanDoren's wide blue eyes made him want to tell her everything. His life story. His past.

She had some kind of weapon in those eyes. They looked all innocent, making him want to believe she was easily led. She wasn't.

"I'm here because Conyers wants to make sure I haven't gone over the edge." The blunt words lay heavy in the air.

"And have you?" Her question was equally blunt, unsurprised.

Was the fact that he had to think about it bad?

The doc stood and rounded her desk, her navy-blue skirt swishing as she walked. She sat on the edge of the chair beside him, but didn't touch him. "Tyler, whatever you say here won't go any further. One of the reasons I have a job is to make sure that our law-enforcement personnel have a safe place to talk about the things that happen to them."

Tyler cleared his throat and made himself lift his eyes from where her skirt slid to show her knees. The words came with some difficulty. "I never crossed the line."

Something in his voice must've given him away. She narrowed her eyes. "Okay."

He fought the urge to elaborate. More words just meant more chances to get himself in trouble. He'd learned that early on in under-cover work. The less said, the better. People either believed you or they didn't.

She smiled and a dimple winked just under the left corner of her lips. *Cute,* that was the word for her. He might've asked her out if things were different.

But, he reminded himself, things *were*

different. And real life harder to slip back into every time he came out from under cover.

The doc rubbed one pink-tipped finger across her bottom lip. "I think I can clear you for work with the department."

Tyler took a deep breath. He could hear the hesitation in her voice. "But…"

"But if you'd like to come in again, the door is always open. Even with breaks, three years is a long time to be undercover."

He had to make a serious effort to calm the resentment that surged at her words and remind himself that he would do what it took because he needed the job.

He needed the time to figure out what he was going to do with the rest of his life. His mother said God had plans for him.

Tyler could just imagine those plans. "I'm fine."

"I'm sure that's true. Let's just make a note to check in while you're readjusting to life on the outside."

He gritted his teeth into a smile. "Sure thing, Doc."

Gracie VanDoren stood. "I'll see you in a day or two?"

She held out a hand to the ex-special agent. He didn't think he'd crossed the line. Between her quick eval and the glowing letters of commendation from his superiors at the DEA, she had no reason to suspect he wouldn't be fine in the field. She just wondered what his definition of "the line" was.

He got to his feet. His hand swallowed hers as he held it. Dark eyes studied hers. "Why wait? Have dinner with me tonight."

She slid her hand from his grasp with a quick smile. "Thank you for the sweet offer, but I don't date."

He leaned a shoulder on the door frame, lady-killer smile spread across his face. "If you don't date cops, that's no problem. I'm not a cop."

"It's not that. I don't date, period." She rounded her desk, putting it between them. The more space the better. She smiled again and picked up the letter opener.

"You don't...really?"

The disbelief on his face would have made her laugh if she hadn't seen dozens of variations of the same look over the past ten years. She chose not to date. Period. She had lots of reasons, but the biggest was that she wanted a real relationship, one built on friendship and trust. Mutual faith.

She ignored the little voice inside that

whispered, *"Yeah, how's that been working out for you?"*

"Let me know if you'd like another appointment." Gracie reached for the stack of mail on her desk yet to be opened. She knew when he left because the room just felt empty. He was something.

He hadn't said anything inconsistent, exactly. No huge waving red flags. He seemed remarkably secure, but there was something in his eyes. It was instinct, really, more than anything concrete that made her think he might want to talk. Just something.

Gracie sighed and picked up another envelope from the precarious stack on her desk. She sliced into it and slid out a single sheet of paper.

Block letters shouted the message: I CAN'T WAIT UNTIL YOU DIE.

Her pulse thudded over the roar in her ears, her breathing short and shallow. Her fingers tightened unconsciously to grip the paper.

"What does it say?" The deep voice came from the door.

She dropped the thing on her desk. Looking up, she met Tyler Clark's too-shrewd brown eyes. She gave herself a second for her heart rate to return to something resembling normal and said, "Nothing. It's just a bill I forgot about. Already back for another appointment?"

He walked closer. "Whatever that is, it isn't 'nothing.' Something in that note scared the daylights out of you. What did it say?"

Gracie pushed the paper toward him. He didn't pick it up, but he scrutinized it. "Is this the first one you've gotten like this?"

She laughed—a quick, non-humorous burst. Without saying a word, she opened a file drawer, pulled out a file and tossed it on her desk. About an inch thick, it held the letters. The phone calls, those were just in her memory.

He flipped through the pages like a deck of cards. "All these?"

"I've testified in the majority of felony cases in this county in the past four years. Most of the offenders think they wouldn't be serving time if it wasn't for me," She shrugged. "I'm a convenient scapegoat. And they send me love letters."

He dropped the stack on the desk. "Is that what they're calling them these days?"

Gracie pursed her lips, giving the file the stink eye. In one way, it was a testimony to the fact that she did her job. In another, it just showed that some people weren't willing to take responsibility for their own actions. Mostly she tended to file the letters and forget them. Yet something about this one sent a shiver of premonition up her spine.

"I need tea."

"What?" Tyler Clark's dark eyebrows drew together.

She hadn't realized that she'd said it out loud. What did that say about her mental health? "Don't you know that a good cup of tea cures everything?"

"Didn't know that, but duly noted. Are you going to give that letter to your CSI team, see if they can figure out where it came from?" He eased a hip onto the corner of her desk. He towered over her, but she was used to that, working in what was still generally a man's world.

"No. It's not necessary."

"You really think that's smart?"

She lifted one shoulder. "I almost always file the letters and never hear from them again. Writing the letter *is* the play for them. Most of them are in prison anyway."

"What about the ones that just got paroled?" Tyler crossed his arms, the fabric of his dress shirt taut against his biceps.

Gracie swallowed hard and leaned back in

her chair. "In cases I testified in, I get a courtesy call from the warden before the inmates are released from custody."

He nodded. "Any calls recently?"

"One or two." Answering his questions, she felt a little like the patient instead of the doctor.

The former agent stood and tucked his hands into the pockets of his boot-cut jeans, his shirt tails hanging loose. Did he know what his attire said about him?

The dress shirt would be considered required, but the jeans and untucked shirt said he wasn't a rule follower. So, she would guess, yes. She smiled up at him.

His face held a toughness, his demeanor an edginess that came from years of living a dangerous double life. But his eyelashes were a black, sooty smudge as he blinked at her. Pretty.

She smiled wider.

"It looks like you have two options, Doc. You can report it to one of the very skilled detectives in the SBPD. Or you can put the paper in your file and forget about it."

Gracie opened her mouth to say she planned to forget it as he said, "I highly suggest option one."

She closed her mouth and scowled. For the first time, she saw a real hint of amusement in Tyler Clark's eyes.

He tilted his head and a dark curl fell across his forehead. "There could be one more option."

"What would that be?" She leaned back in her desk chair and crossed her legs.

"Consulting for the SBPD doesn't exactly fill my day planner. If you'd like to give me the note and the names, I can check it out for you. I have some investigative experience."

Tyler was being modest. The letters she'd read from his superiors at the DEA had been glowing with praise for Tyler's talent as an agent.

She didn't want to be the person who ignored the thing that could've saved her life. She also didn't want to give credence to something she knew from experience was most likely an empty threat. If they followed up on every letter she got, it would be a massive waste of manpower.

Tyler picked up one of Gracie's cards from the holder on her desk. "Gracie? As in 'Amazing'?"

"As in my great-grandmother Graciela.

Tyler, I appreciate your professional input, but you never said why you came back."

Tyler Clark stopped in the motion of tucking her card in his pocket. "You said you don't date, but do you drink coffee?"

Was he challenged by the fact that she didn't date? "I appreciate the offer, but no thanks."

He stood in the door another minute, studying her, his face thoughtful. "Okay, I'll see you around."

As he left, she picked up the threatening letter. The envelope hadn't had the stamp from the prison on the back, so it came from the outside. It wasn't the first, but it was a little unusual.

An involuntary shiver coursed through her. Handling dangerous personalities was part of her job. She took precautions in order to stay safe, but if she'd learned anything in all those interviews, it was this: No one was untouchable.

TWO

Tyler chopped peppers and onions to make fajitas for the crew at his brother Matt's firehouse. He'd timed it strategically for shift change. He'd feed everyone on the A shift, then lay out the spread again for the B shift. He slid the vegetables into a bowl and reached for a ripe avocado.

Another step in the finding-a-life plan. Build relationships with normal people, not drug dealers.

Matt propped his feet on a chair next to Tyler and perused the newspaper. He picked up a pencil to work on the communal crossword puzzle. "So how was your first day at work?"

Tyler sliced around the avocado and gave it an easy twist. "Fine, if you don't mind someone poking around in your brain."

Matt looked up from the crossword puzzle.

"They made you go for a psych eval? With Doc VanDoren?"

Tyler whacked the seed of the avocado with his knife. "Yeah."

As Tyler started mashing the avocado with quick, vicious movements, Matt shoved him from behind with one booted foot. "She got to you, huh?"

"She did not 'get' to me." Tyler started another avocado for the guacamole. Yeah, that was why he couldn't quit thinking about her. "What's her story anyway?"

"She's the real deal as far as I can tell. Why?"

Tyler was absolutely not telling his younger brother that she'd turned him down when he asked her to dinner. He scowled at the unfinished bowl of guacamole and reached for a lime.

Matt eventually gave up on an answer and went back to the paper, shouts from the living room indicating that the video-game war was heating up.

"She really doesn't date." Yes, the words came out of his mouth. While his brother laughed at him, Tyler picked up the squashed lime and took a free-throw shot at the trash can on the other side of the room.

"Look, I can't blame you for trying. She's beautiful, if you go for the Kate Hudson type." Matt was planning a wedding with his former partner in the fire department, Lara Hughes. Something he felt made him a relationship expert.

Tyler pictured the doc with her swishy blue skirt and pretty painted nails. He couldn't see her running into a burning building, either. Didn't mean she wouldn't. She seemed pretty tenacious. Anyone who could go without dating—a thought occurred to him.

"She does like men, right?"

His brother laughed until, red-faced, he gasped for air. "What, she turned you down when you asked her out, so she must not like men?"

Tyler slammed another lime onto the counter to loosen the juices. "That's not what I said."

Matt got up from the chair and dusted off his navy-blue work pants. "Here's a thought. Why don't you ask her to Sunday dinner at Mom and Dad's?" He tossed the paper onto the kitchen table and loped away into the living area.

As much as Tyler hated to admit it, his baby brother had grown up while he'd been away.

Matt was smart, assured and had a faith that Tyler envied. What did Tyler have?

Nightmares.

Questions.

But he could cook. And did, during the long, long nights when he couldn't sleep. The ability to cook had been part of his last cover. His in with the Diablo Brotherhood had been through one of the "brothers" who worked as a sous-chef in a hotel kitchen in Chicago. The DEA had sent Tyler for a crash course at culinary school.

It was one thing he'd done for the DEA that he'd never regretted.

The alarm tones sounded throughout the firehouse. Tyler sighed and turned off the burner, the thud of boots coming from every direction headed toward the engine bay. He sat down at the table and picked up the crossword puzzle. This could take a while.

Gracie paced the lawn of her father's house, now filled with noxious gas fumes. The red lights of the fire trucks flared on the grass in the fading evening light. She didn't live in the main building. No one had since her father died six months ago.

She lived in the pool house. She'd seen the light on in the kitchen when she pulled up. At first she thought perhaps the housekeeper had left it on, but Friday wasn't Mrs. Batterson's day, and a quick call confirmed that.

Immediately upon opening the back door she'd smelled the gas. She paced some more. What could've happened? A pilot light malfunction?

A throat cleared behind her. Matt Clark took a step closer, an easy smile on his face. He looked like his older brother, but not.

"It was probably as simple as turning a burner off, right?"

Matt's expression sobered. "Not exactly. It took us some time to find the leak. A hose inside the stove was damaged. We've turned the gas off at the main valve, but we're going to be here a while airing the place out."

She caught something in his eyes that didn't fit his words. Surely this was a common occurrence for firefighters? "Was the damage caused by use?"

"The line was cut, Doc. Someone wanted the house to fill up with natural gas. As tiny a spark as static electricity could've set it off. You're very lucky."

"Someone cut it?" She was having a hard time believing what she just heard.

"Yes. Have you been in your place yet?"

"No, I smelled the gas and—" The sudden thought that someone might've been in her personal space halted her next words.

Matt's tone was gentle. "Maybe we should check it out."

"Yes. Absolutely. Let me just—find my keys." She dug around in her purse to find the keys that she'd had as she'd opened the door to her father's house. She just couldn't think of it as hers, even though it was, officially speaking.

With Matt and his partner, True, behind her, she walked across the courtyard and around the pool to her little house. One story, with three large sets of French doors across the front, it was created for weekend guests and pool access. She'd converted it into living space after grad school, a compromise with her dad when he'd wanted her home.

Her thoughts were a runaway train, one car chasing right behind the other, imagining what she might find. As she pushed the key toward the lock, or tried, her hand shook and she couldn't get it to slide home so she could unlock the door.

Gracie took one bracing breath and forced the key into the lock. She stepped aside for the two firefighters to enter, each with their masks now in place. They sounded like two robots with their voice magnifiers. She put her hand on Matt's arm. "Will you look for my cat? His name is Charlemagne."

She dropped into one of the lounge chairs by the pool, a brisk breeze off the bay lifting her hair, sending a chill over her skin. She pulled the lapels of her short jacket across her chest. Not normally given to panic, she'd kind of lost it over the thought that someone had been in her house.

Matt walked out her front door. "It looks good. True is checking the stove, the outlets and probably the attic, too, but there's definitely no gas smell in there, not like in the house. I fed your cat. He was a little ticked off."

She took a deep breath and laughed, realizing for the first time just how freaked she really had been. "Thanks, Matt. I don't like the idea that someone's been in my dad's house. And I really didn't like the thought that they may have broken into my house, too."

"We didn't see any evidence that your house—your dad's house—had been broken in to." The firefighter turned his helmet in his hands.

Gracie turned the ramifications of his statement in her mind. "Do you think I'm not safe in my own home?"

Matt shrugged. "That's really not a question I can answer."

The uneasiness she'd felt came surging back. "Is it okay for me to go inside and pack a bag? I think I'll go to a hotel tonight just to give me some time to think this through."

"That's a good idea. And yes, it's fine. I'll give True the heads-up."

Gracie slipped her purse strap over her shoulder as she walked toward her little cottage. She loved the light airy blue and apple-green walls, the bright blue pops of color that the throw pillows provided on her white furniture. Charlemagne twined between her legs, bumping his big head on her calves. She'd always felt so cozy and safe here, in direct opposition to how she felt in the main estate house, which was so big and so empty without her dad. That someone could take that feeling away from her made her sad and more than a little angry.

And determined. She would find out who was doing this to her. No one had the right to control her actions, except her.

Tyler's watch said eight thirty a.m. If he had to guess, the very perky Dr. VanDoren was an early riser.

He knocked on the door of the hotel room.

Her muffled request came from behind the door and he dug around for his wallet, flipping it open to his retired DEA ID. He held it up to the peephole.

The locks disengaged and her pretty blue eyes appeared in the crack. "How did you find me?"

He quirked an eyebrow.

"Right—Matt." She opened the door wider to reveal a sumptuous suite of rooms.

"Slumming it, are we?" He nodded behind her.

She glanced back but didn't take the bait. She also didn't invite him in.

He leaned against the door frame and she edged back. She looked different today, her legs encased in long slim denim.

The silence dragged. The doc crossed her arms. "Is there something I can help you with, Tyler?"

"You eat, right?" At her brief nod, he barreled on. "I came to see if you wanted to go get breakfast."

She shook her head. "You don't know when to give up, do you? I'm not going out with you, Tyler."

"Oh, I forgot to tell you. It's not a date."

Her eyes met his again. "It's not?"

He tilted his head toward the parking lot. "Only if you think taking a thirteen-year-old to breakfast is a date."

She walked to the rail and peered over. A middle-school boy with tight brown curls and a hoodie waved up at her. "Where'd you get him?"

Tyler laughed out loud. The woman sure was suspicious. He loved it. "I didn't 'get' him anywhere. That's my little brother, Marcus. I was gone for three years. Saturday breakfast seems like the least I can do to get to know the kid."

"Making up for lost time?" Her voice was soft...sweet.

"Trying."

From the parking lot, a voice drifted up. "Come on, man, what's taking you so long? Get the girl and let's go. I'm starving."

Tyler grinned. "Charming, isn't he?"

"Give me just a minute to grab a jacket." She disappeared into the hotel suite and came back moments later with a bright green twill jacket. With her multicolored striped shirt, she was a bright spot of color on an otherwise overcast day.

At his truck, she held out a hand to Marcus. "I'm Dr. VanDoren, but my friends call me

Gracie." She caught Tyler's quick sidelong glance at the nickname. "Thanks for letting me go along today."

"I'm Marcus. You should stick with me. I'm obviously better with women than he is." He shot a look at his older brother, and Gracie laughed as Marcus held the door open for her.

Marcus didn't stop talking the whole five minutes it took to get to the coffee shop. "I like to go to the Worldwide House of Waffles, but Tyler went to school with the people who own this place, so we have to eat here."

"Which is such a hardship for you because the food is terrible." Tyler shot back at Marcus.

"Yep." Marcus grinned at Gracie.

At Sip This, Tyler held the door of the big Ford open for Gracie as she slid to the ground. She didn't wobble, but still, she reached for the hand Marcus held out to her. "Thanks, this truck is really high."

Inside, Tyler found them a table against the wall. "I'll go order. Scrambled egg on an English muffin for Marcus and blueberry scones for us. Okay?"

Gracie nodded. "And tea. Earl Grey."

"This is a coffee shop, Gracie."

"And the proprietor, Sailor, likes good tea. Earl Grey, please." Gracie gave him the look she usually reserved for recalcitrant patients.

He smiled. "At your service, ladies."

"He's so annoying." Marcus kicked back in the chair, letting it bump against the wall. "Don't let him bug you."

"I won't, but thanks." She looked at Marcus. He was a gorgeous kid—creamy brown skin and dark, soulful eyes. His attitude certainly matched those of his brothers. She could see why Tyler's mother would've been drawn to him. "So, how old were you when you were adopted?"

"What? I'm adopted?" Instantly, those eyes filled, one tear clinging to his lower lashes where they curved to meet his cheek.

Her stomach plummeted.

He grinned. "I'm just kidding."

She shook her head, rolling her eyes at him. "Another five seconds and I'd have figured that out on my own, but thanks for making me lose my appetite."

"I was adopted when I was ten. My foster parents pretty much left me at the hospital when they found out I had diabetes, and Mom—Mrs. C—well, first she was really ticked off, and then she brought me home."

He smiled again, this time a sweet curve as his face lit up with the memory.

"You never met Tyler then, because he was away when you were adopted."

"Yep."

No wonder Tyler was so determined to make things up to this kid. He probably hadn't even known about him. She looked at Tyler as he chatted with Gabe, the owner's husband. He glanced back at her and gave her a little half smile as Gabe slid their order to him.

Tyler dropped into his chair. "What'd I miss?"

"Your girlfriend made me cry."

Gracie thoroughly enjoyed breakfast out with two manly men from the Clark family, although it took every bit of mental stamina to hang in there with them. She really needed to meet their mother. The woman had to be a saint.

As they turned into a driveway, she looked up, startled. "Tyler, this is my house. Not the hotel."

"I know. Matt said the guys were working all night airing the place out. It's safe to enter, and I figured you'd want to take a look."

That lovely scone she'd eaten turned in her

stomach. Did she want to take a look? She wasn't sure.

A skeleton crew of firefighters remained, but they were rolling up an extension cord getting ready to remove the last of the gigantic fans they'd used to clear the air at her father's house.

She walked in the kitchen door, and Tyler stepped in behind her. She waited for his inevitable comment on the place, the obvious expense of top-of-the-line everything. From Italian marble countertops to the La Cornue stove, the kitchen was the tip of the iceberg, a gourmet cook's dream.

Tyler didn't say a word—only ran a finger down the pricey stove. "I'm going to look around."

She'd seen literally dozens of cops in her career, but she couldn't think of a one she'd rather have in her house with her right now. That "I mean business" look certainly had its appeal in a situation like this.

Gracie looked around the living room. Everything looked the same. Would she even notice if something were out of place? Maybe not. The family room upstairs had been her domain when she lived here, where she and her father had spent time together the rare times when he'd been home.

The living area curved into a hall that led to her dad's study. The leather furniture and dark cherry paneling gave the room a cozy, rich feeling even on an overcast winter day. All she needed was a fire. She reached for the switch by the fireplace.

And jerked her hand back. Someone had wanted to blow the house up. With gas. Turning on the gas fireplace probably wouldn't be a good idea.

As a little girl, their house was magical, and in some ways, it still was. The memories were still there. Memories of having breakfast with her mom on the terrace, or her dad tucking her into bed when he got home from work. But it didn't feel like hers, not anymore.

She'd loved her father intensely. After her mother died when she was thirteen, her dad was all she had.

Gracie sat in his desk chair and looked over the surface of the desk, still with a few of her dad's papers on it. She lifted one and dropped it. It had been six months.

Maybe it was time to throw them away. Or at least file them. She would tell herself avoidance wasn't healthy if she had herself as a patient.

Tyler knocked on the door frame. "Mind if I come in?"

"Not at all." She leaned back in the cushy leather chair. "Where's Marcus?"

"Knowing that kid, he's probably down at the water picking up hermit crabs and getting soaking wet."

She laughed. "The water's still freezing."

"Yeah, well. He's thirteen and male. I don't think his nerve endings have kicked in yet." His eyes quickly sobered, narrowing in concentration. "How was your relationship with your dad?"

Gracie crossed her arms. "I don't understand what that has to do with anything."

"I'm not sure it does, but I found this in a trash can upstairs." He tossed a couple of pieces of paper onto the desk.

She hesitated as she reached for the torn pieces. She didn't really want to touch them, her fingers inexplicably numb.

"It's from our trip to Wyoming." She'd been fourteen. They'd gone to see Old Faithful and camped overnight in Yellowstone, and this had been her favorite photo. In fact, she had one just like it on a bookshelf in her bedroom.

"He traveled a lot. I only went on a couple of trips with him. Most of the time I stayed behind with Mrs. Batterson—but this trip was special. It wasn't a business trip. It was just for the two of us."

"You look happy."

She ran her finger over the ragged edge of the tear between her and her dad. "I was. He was focused on me. There are only a few times I can say it was like that...because he was gone so much." Gracie looked at Tyler. "Who would do this?"

He looked at her. "I guess we start with who has access to the house. Can you make me a list?"

"Sure." She pulled open a drawer to look for a piece of paper, shaking her hands, trying to get feeling back to her fingers. The house was chilly from being open all night, the high ceilings making it hard to heat, even in the spring.

"You're shivering. You can make the list at the hotel. If you give me your key I'll check out the rest of this place and yours. Barring any complications, you'll be back here, if not tomorrow, Monday."

Tyler Clark with his dark eyes and bad-boy charm may not have looked like your typical white knight, but he'd turned out to be her champion today. "Why so long?"

He shook his head. "The cut in the tubing of the stove was hard to find, even though Matt and his crew knew to look for it. I want to search everything carefully, make sure there are no other surprises."

As they walked through the living room, Gracie glanced up the stairs. The house was so big. So empty. It needed life—people—to make it feel like a home.

She tried to imagine someone coming in and cutting the tubing in the stove in the kitchen and couldn't imagine why someone would want to destroy this house.

Gracie shivered again and rubbed her arms.

Because whether the attack was meant for the house or for her, she was most definitely the target.

THREE

Tyler strolled into the police precinct on Monday at eight a.m. per Captain Cruse Conyers's orders. He didn't know why Conyers had ordered him in, only that he'd been expected to be there.

He shifted the ball cap on his head, lowering it just a smidge over his eyes, trying not to catch the attention of any particular person in the room. He knew a couple of the guys, at least to say hello, but he didn't want to stop and hash out the drug case they'd just closed.

He knocked on the captain's door. Cruse waved him in as he hung up the phone.

"Have a seat." Cruse stretched his hands over his head and locked his fingers behind his neck.

"What's up? If this is about the psych eval, the doc passed me."

"It's not about that. I talked to Gracie. I

know you're good to go. In fact, that's why I called you in." Cruse's laser-sharp green eyes took in everything from Tyler's ragged ball cap to his brand-new Nikes.

"Our consult is scheduled for next week, but if you need to move it up—"

"No, but I need a favor. It's weird, but there's been an outbreak of chicken pox at the high school, and our resource officer—"

"I'm not going to work at the high school." Tyler didn't raise his voice, but he used every bit of drug dealer menace he'd learned over the past five years in the DEA.

Surprise tinged Cruse's features, but he laughed. "No way would I inflict you on hapless teenagers." He stopped and considered. "Although, an ex-DEA agent in the high school might put a stop to that group of cheerleaders who insists on smoking weed in the bathrooms."

"No."

Cruse laughed again. "Don't worry, I've got the high school covered. The officer who worked the high school before Rodriguez is going to be there this week, but that leaves me with a hole in my patrol."

"And you're thinking I could fill it?" Tyler raised a skeptical eyebrow. He wasn't a beat cop.

He wasn't a cop at all.

"Why not? You're a cop."

Tyler stared at Cruse from under the bill of his cap.

Cruse ticked off his fingers. "You've been to FLETC, you have field experience and you have advanced lifesaving skills, always a plus."

"Federal law-enforcement training doesn't teach you much about being a cop in the field." He relaxed against the chair, crossing his ankle over the other knee.

"You have good instincts, Tyler. I saw that when we worked together on the Bright Orange drug case. You knew when that thing was about to blow wide open and when it was time to move. I could really use someone with your skills on this team for good."

"Look—Cruse. I appreciate what you're trying to do, but I never wanted to do local police work." Something his dad had never understood. His dad really never understood anything about him, about his need to leave home, to make a difference in his own way. He needed to make peace with his dad, but that was a step in the get-a-life-plan that he wasn't quite ready for yet.

Apparently realizing that arguing would be futile, Cruse held his hands up. "Well, it was worth a shot. If you change your mind—"

"I won't." Tyler cut in. "But thanks. And your resource officer?"

Cruse grinned. "He really does have the chicken pox, poor kid."

The phone rang, and as Cruse reached for it Tyler stood. "Thanks again, Cruse. I appreciate the compliment."

Conyers gave a short nod. "Anytime."

Tyler left the police precinct and turned his big truck toward the bay. The breeze had kicked up a light chop on the water, and the sun, bright in a clear sky, glinted on it like tiny diamonds. Even with the tourist traffic, it was only minutes to Gracie's estate.

He hadn't missed that she always referred to the big house as her father's. The research he'd done last night after he got back to the condo he was renting wasn't exactly revealing. Her dad had made a lot of money in real estate development along the Gulf Coast and in Sedona and Scottsdale, Arizona.

He'd left everything to Gracie.

Gracie, who had a huge estate with an

unbelievable La Cornue stove and who chose to live in the pool house.

Gracie, who didn't date. At all.

She was a mystery. And so was the fact that someone had broken into her house and cut the gas line. In his opinion, it was obvious that whoever it was had been after her.

The good news was, they didn't know her personally or they would know she didn't live in the mansion. Who would live in the pool house when they owned that huge house?

What didn't make sense was the torn picture. If one of the people she'd sent to jail had gotten out and decided to come after her, why would he tear up a picture of her and her dad? Why not one of the pictures of Gracie alone? Or if revenge was the motive, why not all the photos?

He turned down the winding road to the house. It was pretty—not manicured, exactly, though he could tell that some flowering trees had been planted in strategic places along the way. It would be beautiful in a week or two.

Looking objectively at the house, its Mediterranean style was appealing. But with no one living there, it looked empty—out of place.

Like he felt being back in "real life." He'd known it would take time to adjust to life on the outside again. He hadn't known it would be this hard. Sometimes he felt like people were speaking a foreign language, words he didn't know. Emotions he remembered but didn't recall how to feel or harness.

He jammed the truck into park and got out, slamming the door behind him. The soft, salty air felt good on his face. He didn't know what he wanted to do with his life, such as it was. He'd been a criminal so long, he didn't know how to be a good guy.

But he knew how to help Gracie.

And as far as he could tell, she was in over her head, with no idea where to look for help.

Lunchtime Monday, Gracie pulled up at her house with two steaming grouper sandwiches and a bag of baked pita chips. She had some roasted pepper hummus in the fridge that she could pull out to round out the lunch. She figured that since Tyler was blowing two whole days to check out her house, the least she could do was feed him.

It wasn't a date. It was her bringing lunch to someone helping her out. Totally different.

She found him in the pool house with his head under the sink. "Everything okay under there?"

A thump and a muffled word or two came from under the sink before she saw Tyler's dark head. "Fine. Thanks for asking."

"I have lunch. I set it up poolside."

He'd rolled up his shirtsleeves over a long-sleeved T-shirt. He looked like a workman. But then, she guessed that was a talent in itself, learning to blend in.

She grabbed the hummus and a couple of sodas from the refrigerator and met Tyler at the glass-topped table by the pool.

He'd already pulled a sandwich out of the bag and glanced up at her. "Sure you don't want to eat inside? It's still a little chilly out here."

"I've got my jacket, and it's a beautiful day." She didn't mention that she'd never had a man in her house before.

"This is kinda like a lunch date, you and me." He made the connection. She should've known he would. "Guess that's why we're out here and not in there?"

She opened her sandwich and spread the paper on the glass tabletop. "I like it out here."

Tyler took a big bite of his sandwich and made an appreciative noise.

"Good?"

"Really good. The fish could use just a little something though. Maybe a hint of dill?" He took another bite.

She took another bite of her sandwich to cover her confusion. There was a lot more to Tyler Clark than she first suspected. "So, you cook?"

"Went to culinary school courtesy of the DEA." He popped open the hummus and dug a pita chip into it.

"How long were you away?" She stopped eating. He was more interesting than her sandwich.

"About five years total, give or take. At first I was still able to come home for visits, but when the undercover job came up, I had to cut off contact with my family." He looked across the yard to the water, glinting in the sun.

"That was hard for you?"

"It was easier than it should've been." His voice was sad, a hint of longing there that she couldn't quite put her finger on.

"And coming home?"

"Harder than it should be." He wasn't looking at her, only scowling at his sandwich.

"I'm sorry—it should be the opposite. Your mom sounds like a really nice lady."

"She is. She's great. And my dad's a good

guy, just old school. It's his way or the high-way, I guess." The breeze rattled the paper off the sandwiches. Tyler put his drink on it as it skidded across the table.

"So you took the highway."

He smiled—a rarity from him. "Yeah, I guess I did. Thanks for the session, Doc. I guess this wasn't a date after all."

"I don't date, Tyler."

"Why not? I know for a fact it's not because you haven't had chances." He raised his eyes from the table to meet hers. Dark eyes, the color of espresso beans, framed by thick black lashes. He had a way of looking at her, paying attention to what she was saying, listening. She'd listened to a lot of people in her life and career, but had anyone ever really listened to her?

She reached under her shirt and pulled out a chain with a ring on it. "It says, *Worth the wait*. My dad had it made for me when I was thirteen. He said that true love is worth wait-ing for and that the person to marry is your best friend. You don't need dates for that."

She chewed on her bottom lip while she waited for him to say something. She so seldom talked about her reasons for not dating.

Most people didn't ask, figuring it was a bad breakup, or something.

It didn't matter what he thought. She knew what was the right thing for her. God desired for her to have a full and happy marriage. She didn't believe that dating, especially the way most of her friends dated, was the right way to get there. At least it wasn't the way God wanted her to find her spouse.

And if that made her a freak, well, it was a shame, but it wouldn't change her mind. Only God could do that.

"Don't you have anything to say?"

Tyler popped the last bite of his sandwich into his mouth. "Nope, not really. I guess I figure if you're brave enough to take a stand like that, then I'm man enough not to give you a hard time about it."

He stood and picked up his trash, then put it down again, digging in his jeans pocket. He pulled out a tiny round black thing and tossed it on the table. "I almost forgot. I found that in the master bedroom in the main house. I didn't find more, but that doesn't mean there aren't others."

She reached for it and then pulled her hand back. "What is it?"

"A bug?" He tipped it with his finger and

sent it rolling. "It's wireless, the kind you can buy at pretty much any electronics store. It probably means that whoever is listening is only listening periodically. They'd have to be close."

"There was someone in my father's house, that planted that thing?" Her usual calm deserted her. For some reason the idea that someone might've been listening to her most private moments was worse than the idea that someone had tried to blow her up.

He nodded.

A burning resentment was starting to grow in her belly. "Did you find any in the pool house?"

"No. I haven't looked everywhere yet, though. And just to be safe, I've called in a friend, someone who happens to be really good at finding these things."

"Someone from the DEA?"

"Uh, no."

She clenched her fist around the tiny device. "I can't believe this. Why? Why would someone bug my house?"

He slid his big, warm hand under her fist and one by one peeled back her cold fingers until the bug dropped into his hand. "I'll take care of this, Gracie. If you let me."

As he turned to walk away, he brushed his fingers across her knuckles. Just that.

Her breath hitched. She had to make herself take another one.

Houses rigged to blow up, listening devices and six-foot-something of ex-DEA danger.

She was in so much trouble.

FOUR

Tyler rounded a curve in the thick woods around Gracie's house. She'd gone back to work a half hour ago, and he'd started the search on the east side of her property but had backtracked now to come out on the other side. He hadn't found anything but a bunch of briars and a sleepy snake.

After a few more careful steps, he caught sight of a patch of color that didn't quite match the mottled blur of the forest. He moved closer. A vehicle was pulled into the thick underbrush.

The van looked old—peeling two-tone brown paint and rust spots nearly covered the surface. It looked like it could fall in at any moment. Its tires, however, were a different story. Those were brand new, a dead giveaway that this vehicle was not what it appeared to be. Another, slightly less obvious sign, was the antenna sticking out of a back window. Oh, yeah.

He walked a three-sided perimeter and, as he reached the driver's side, saw a shadowy figure. He opened his phone and punched in a text to Detective Joe Sheehan, who had been very interested when Tyler told him about finding the bug in Gracie's house.

Step by quiet, painstaking step, he made his way back to the passenger side. In one smooth motion, he charged the van, opened the door and slid into the passenger seat.

The driver tried to jump out the other side. Tyler grabbed the man's arm, wrenching it behind him.

"Stop, stop. I won't run." The driver yammered the words as Tyler tightened the pressure.

Fortyish, in jeans and a polo, the guy looked unremarkable, like he'd fit in pretty much anywhere in middle America, even with what looked like a barbecue stain on the yellow shirt. He smoothed the shirt as Tyler let him go. "Who are you?"

The man reached and Tyler made a sharp move toward him, putting a firm hand on his chest.

"Just going for my wallet. Man, you're jumpy."

"You're trespassing. Pull out the ID with two fingers."

Slowly, with one hand in the air, and using the two first fingers of the other hand, the man pulled his wallet out of his back pocket and handed it to Tyler. Tyler flipped it open and studied it for a second. "So, Walter Montgomery, private investigator, why are you bugging the house down the street?"

"I'm not—" Walter cut his eyes to catch Tyler's expression and glanced down at the sound equipment in his lap. "Okay, I am, but it's just a job. Find out what the girl does, what she wears, eats, where she gets her hair done. Totally harmless background stuff."

"For who?"

"I can't tell you that." Walter's voice had gone up two octaves. "Word gets around I can't be trusted and my career is toast."

Tyler looked into the back of the van at the sleeping bag and hot plate. A tiny TV/DVD combo sat in one corner. The whole vehicle smelled like old banana peels and coffee. Some career. "How much are you getting paid?"

"I make decent money, you just don't worry

about that." Walter sniffed and stuck his wallet back in his pocket.

"I'm sure you do fine, Walter. I didn't mean to insult your manhood." He reached in his pocket and, from his wallet, pulled five twenty-dollar bills. "I'd like to ask you a few questions. I like your answers, you get the money. I don't, I keep it."

Walter's Adam's apple bobbed, his eyes on the money. "Okay, sure."

He'd start with an easy one. "Where are you from?"

"Biloxi, Mississippi."

Tyler nodded. With the casinos in Biloxi, it made sense that there would be more than one private investigator in that tiny town. Located two states over, it was still within easy driving distance of Sea Breeze.

"Who hired you?"

"I don't know."

Tyler pulled a twenty off the stack and shoved it back in his pocket.

Walter chewed his bottom lip. "Okay, okay. I have an email address. It's one of those generic ones, so I don't think you're gonna get very far with it, but you can have it."

"I want the phone number you have, too."

Tyler tapped the four remaining twenty-dollar bills.

With a reluctant sigh, Walter pulled out his cell phone and scrolled until he found a number and held it up so Tyler could see it. "I don't think you're going to have much luck with this either. I'm not stupid—I ran the number. It's a throwaway and she only uses it to call me. It's never been on when I've tried to call her."

She and *her.* So Walter did know something about the person who hired him. Tyler tucked that tidbit into the back of his mind to mull over later. "How long have you been doing this surveillance?"

"A little over a week. I've followed the girl a couple of places, but she's pretty boring. When I wasn't getting much after a couple of days, I set the bugs and left."

Tyler wasn't touching that statement. The police were going to want to talk to Walter. They'd want to know whether he went back into the house and what he heard when the gas line was cut, provided that he wasn't the one who did it...

As he handed the money to Walter, two police cars pulled forward and blocked the van in place, blue-and-reds flashing. "You've been very cooperative, Walter. I hope you'll be as helpful to my friends."

"What frien—aww, man." Walter's voice climbed, the whites of his eyes gleaming as he searched in vain for an escape route.

"Don't make this harder. It doesn't have to go badly for you if you cooperate." Tyler didn't move as two uniform cops walked toward the van, one on either side.

"That's real easy for you to say. Thanks a lot." Walter put his hands on the wheel where the cops could see them.

Tyler smiled. "See you around, Walter."

He shook his head. It would be a simple matter to get rid of the bugs Walter had planted. Less simple to figure out who was behind hiring Walter in the first place. Tyler looked down at the slip of paper in his hand. He did have a starting place.

Gracie bumped—literally—into Maria Fuentes Storm at the elevator, as she was digging in her bag for the key to her office. "I'm so sorry, Maria. I get the klutz award for the day."

The CSI chief grinned over a yawn. "No problem. I wasn't watching either. Crime scene call-out at two a.m. I think I'm asleep standing up."

"I don't know how you do it." Maria had a new husband and a five-year-old little boy that she'd adopted when they gotten married.

"Lots and lots of caffeine. Hey, I got the preliminary results back on the hair the guys found at your place." The elevator doors opened and Maria stepped on. "It's from a female."

DNA? Gracie walked onto the elevator. "I didn't know you were testing any evidence."

"The cops on-scene brought in a few things for us to process. The one thing that was interesting was blood evidence on the cut tubing itself."

"Are you sure that it wasn't old? Couldn't it have been mine, or the housekeeper's?"

"It wasn't your blood type." Maria stepped off the elevator onto her floor. "I'll keep you posted."

Gracie got off the elevator at her own floor, her mind still on the hair at the house. She nearly bumped into Tyler at the door to her office.

Long and lean, the hard edge of his undercover work still on his face, Tyler leaned against the wall by her door, a ball cap pulled low over his eyes.

"What are you doing here, Tyler? Didn't I just leave you?"

He shrugged. "I came to see you. Thought you might want to know I caught the guy who bugged your house."

"Where?" The word shot out like the report of a gun.

"In the woods, near your house. I told you he would be close. I was right."

"What about the devices inside the house?"

"Relax, my guy is there getting rid of them." He peered at her from underneath his lashes. "So, what's eating at you?"

She stared at his dark eyes, seeing herself mirrored in the depths. "Maria said they're testing DNA. The preliminary reports tell them it's from a female, not me."

Tyler had been leaning toward her, but he took a step back, lounged against the wall and crossed his legs. "Is that right?"

"You know something." She narrowed her eyes. "Spill it."

The ease with which she read him was astonishing, considering that he was alive because of his ability to keep things to himself. "It's not much. The private investigator didn't know who hired him, but he did know it was a female. So I'd say the place to start would be—"

"My threat file." She opened the door to her office. "There haven't been as many women as men—and the majority of those are probably still in prison, so that narrows it down even more." She picked the hefty file up from her desk and promptly dropped it, scattering papers all over the floor.

"Hey." Tyler came toward her, his long denim-clad legs crossing the room in two steps.

She dropped to her knees to pick up the scattered papers.

He followed her to the floor and put his hands over hers. "We'll figure this out. I promise."

She sat back on her heels as her phone beeped from inside her big yellow purse. She grabbed for it and stuck her hand into its buttery leather depths. Searching, she closed her fingers over the phone. She held Tyler's eyes as she punched the button. "Hi, Cruse. What's up?"

She dug in her bag again, firing rapid questions at her boss, who didn't have nearly enough answers for a hostage situation. She scribbled Cruse's answers onto the notepad that she managed to scrounge from her bag.

Three hostages. Father, hostage taker. Two little girls.

Divorce final while deployed overseas. Worked his way here from North Carolina. Her stomach plummeted as he gave her the final facts.

"That's it, that's all you can give me?" She pulled car keys out of her bag and started toward the door.

"We'll know more once you get on-scene," Cruse said. "Right now, the hostage taker is refusing to talk to anyone. I'm hoping you can change that. Here's the address."

She jotted the address onto the notepad. "Okay, I'll be there as soon as possible. But, Cruse, because of the military experience and the recent divorce, you might want to consider using Joe to negotiate."

Gracie clicked off and bumped into the solid wall of Tyler.

"I'll drive."

"Tyler, I don't have time to argue with you. You're a civilian—you need to stay out of this." He flinched, and she felt a smidgeon of guilt.

"Gracie, I know those little girls, Tabitha and Shandy. That address—it's a duplex.

My brother owns it, lives next door. What happened?"

"A neighbor called it in. She saw a man approach the little girls in the yard." She took a breath. "Tyler, Matt's inside with them."

His chest clutched in fear, even as he told himself it would be okay. His brother was smart. He knew how to handle himself. "My truck's right downstairs. I'll get you to the scene."

Instead of arguing, she nodded and followed Tyler down the stairs. In the parking lot, she slid into the passenger seat of his truck and buckled her seat belt, looking over the scant few notes she had.

Tyler surged into the line of spring-break traffic. A horn blared. He ignored it. "Are you always called in a situation like this?"

"Yes. We don't have a SWAT team—our police force is too small—but a few years back, we put together a Crisis Response Team with the county and a couple of neighboring towns. We train together every month and once a year with the FBI at Quantico."

Her phone rang again and she punched the button. "VanDoren…yes. Definitely. Find out where he was deployed last and find his C.O. Our ETA is…"

Tyler held up two fingers.

"Two minutes." She clicked off. "Tyler, I know you're worried."

"I am, but Matt's smart. He'll be fine." Tyler had to believe it. He'd barely slowed the car to a stop before Gracie was out of it, running toward the barricade. She was really something, another of her silky skirts swishing around her knees, plowing through the barricade of cops, her high heels tattooing a rhythm on the pavement. She'd been upset this morning—he'd seen it in her eyes—and yet, when the situation called for it, she was able to put it aside.

Whether she realized it or not, she was a good cop.

Tyler strode up to the barricade and spoke to the officer with the clipboard. "Tyler Clark. I'm family. My brother's one of the hostages."

"I'm sorry, sir. I can't let you through."

"It's fine, Officer. He's with me." Captain Conyers stepped up to the barricade. The uniformed cop lifted the tape to let Tyler pass as Cruse continued, "I'm not sure this is your area of expertise."

"I know, but maybe there's something I can help with." He spread his hands in appeal. "Cruse. It's my brother."

Cruse stopped in front of the door to the neighbor's house, which would've been evacuated by now. With Tyler right behind him, he pushed through the small group of techs and cops, stopping in front of a large picture window.

A recorder and computers had been set up on a table, a makeshift operations command center. "When are we going to call again?"

Gracie looked up from her seat at the table. "Two minutes. Joe?"

"He's deep-sea fishing twenty miles out. He's not going to make it. It's all yours."

The captain turned back to Tyler. "You stay, but keep out of the way. Alisha Lane—the wife—do you know where she works?" At Tyler's nod, Cruse pointed to the uniformed officer standing at the door. "Tell him. We need her here an hour ago."

Tyler gave the officer what little information he had. Alisha Lane worked a shift at the hospital. If his brother was watching the girls, that's probably where she would be. But according to the cop, she wasn't answering her phone.

Gracie glanced up. A knot of fear and frustration lodged somewhere around his diaphragm. Because he could see in those pretty blue eyes just how tricky it was going to be to get them out alive.

FIVE

Gracie put on headphones so she could hear every nuance of the hostage taker's voice, while behind her, Cruse Conyers did the same. As much as she wanted to be a friend to Tyler because he had been one for her, the best way she could help him in this situation was to do her job.

"Okay, we're not going to keep him waiting." She picked up the phone and pressed the recorder, while behind them Cruse Conyers did the same.

In the room, the phone rang once, twice, three times before it was finally picked up.

"Would you please quit calling here?" The hostage taker's voice trembled with stress.

"Mr. Lane, my name is Gracie. I'm with the Sea Breeze Police Depart—" She cut off as the hostage taker interrupted.

"Are you outside my house?"

"Yes, Mr. Lane, we're outside the house. We're here to help you. Is everyone okay in there?"

She could hear one of the twins crying in the background.

He hesitated for a second but said, "Yeah, everyone's fine. These are my girls. I'm taking care of them."

Tricky territory here, but with no visuals, she had to ask. "And their babysitter? Matt?"

"Still breathing, unfortunately."

She let out a breath—she'd have to come back to that. She needed to build a rapport with Lane. "I have your name wrong, don't I? It's Sergeant Lane, isn't it?"

There was a long moment of silence over the speaker. "I served my country."

"Sergeant Lane, is there anything I can get for you? Do you need anything?"

"Just to be left alone. They're *my* kids. I need for you to let me take care of my girls. Can you back off and let me do that?"

Gracie looked out the window at the silent house across the street, the power having been cut as soon as CRT made the scene. "I'll be happy to give you some time like you asked, but first I need to know we can work together.

The girls are scared, Sergeant Lane. I know you don't want to scare your little girls. Why don't you let them come out here and then we'll give you some time to work this out?"

"No! They're my girls. I promised them we'd be together. All I wanted when I got home was to have my family back." He hissed out a breath. "And what do I get instead? Divorce papers in Afghanistan. Is that fair?"

It wasn't a good sign that he was talking about past events. They wanted him thinking about planning a future. But he was also thinking about promises broken. She filed that in the back of her mind, for now.

"I can see why you'd be upset, Daniel."

"How could you possibly understand?" The former Marine's voice climbed, agitation clearly audible now.

"I can't, Daniel. Can I call you Daniel?" She took a sip from the water bottle on the table in front of her. "I can't truly understand because I haven't been where you have. But I can see how the memory of your family—the memory of what you're fighting to get home to—how that would be the thing that keeps you going over there."

Daniel Lane didn't speak.

She glanced at Cruse, who shrugged. "I

know it must be hard to come home and find out what you thought you were coming home to isn't what you thought it would be. But you're Tabitha and Shandy's daddy. No one can change that." A note of urgency filled her voice. "Those little girls need *you*. Let it be about them."

"This *is* about them." Alisha Lane's ex-husband slammed the phone down.

Gracie slumped back against the hard metal chair, pinching the spot that ached between her eyebrows. "That could've gone better. But I think it was the right thing to try to give him a reason to move forward."

Cruse nodded. "You did fine. Something to build on."

"What do we know about this guy? Where has he been since he's been back stateside?" She pushed away from the table just as Alisha Lane burst into the room. Frantic, the twins' mother looked from one person to the other until she reached a face she knew.

"Tyler, what's going on here? Where are my babies?" She trembled uncontrollably, her big brown eyes brimming with tears.

"Your ex-husband is holding them in your house, Alisha." He said it quick and clean, and as her legs sagged, he caught her. His expression, raw with fear and compassion, slayed Gracie.

She knelt in front of the young mother. "Alisha, I'm Gracie VanDoren. I help the police department in cases like this. We need your help to understand Daniel." She caught her gaze. "Is there anything you can give us that might reach him, maybe sway him to come out?"

"He wasn't the same person after the first deployment. I was afraid of him. I tried to talk to him about getting some help, but he wouldn't even consider it. When he deployed the last time, I filed for divorce and moved here." Her eyes filled with tears again as she looked at Tyler. "He's not a bad person. The things he saw—things he had to do—they changed him."

"Believe me, I get it." Tyler's face didn't change, but his voice was hoarse. Of course, he would understand.

"Four minutes," one of the techs called out.

The twins' mom shook from head to toe.

Gracie reached for her hand and remembered Daniel's comment about broken promises. "Is there anything he ever said he would do and didn't get the chance to? A promise, even a silly one, that he made to you or the girls?"

Alisha chewed on her lip. "I'm sorry, I just can't think, knowing they're over there in that house with him. And Matt—I'm so sorry, Tyler."

"You know, given the choice, Matt would want to be in there with Tabitha and Shandy."

"Hey, Doc, one of the uniforms found the guy's car. It's parked about two blocks away. It looks like he's been living in it. And these were in there." Todd, a member of the Crisis Response Team, handed her a nearly empty bottle of caffeine pills.

"Okay, that helps understand his mental status." It didn't help their situation, but that was out of her control. She looked at her watch. "It's about time to give him another call, let him know we haven't forgotten he's in there."

"Wait—Dr. VanDoren, I'm not sure if this is what you're talking about, but Daniel promised the girls he would get them a puppy when he got home. They were still so little when he left, but they might remember." The mom's face held a mixture of hope and fear.

Gracie gave Alisha's hand a squeeze. "That's

great. Exactly the kind of thing I was looking for. Okay, time for me to get back to work."

As she walked away, the young mother's voice stopped her. "They're going to be okay, right?"

Tyler wrapped his arm around Alisha's thin shoulders. "They're good at what they do, Alisha. Matt and your girls are in good hands. But we can—" He stumbled a little on the words and Gracie's heart stumbled with him. "We can pray."

When the young mom nodded and closed her eyes, Tyler bowed his head close to hers. Gracie couldn't hear the words, but she could see his lips moving as he prayed for the safety of his brother and two little girls they both loved.

Tyler watched Gracie slide into her seat. On the phone with Alisha's ex-husband once again, she talked quietly, persuasively. And Tyler could only pray that she was getting through, that the wedding celebration they were planning for Matt and Lara would still be a celebration.

Just behind the police staging area, he could see the ambulance on stand-by. Lara was on duty today. He wondered where she was, if she was somewhere behind the tape praying for Matt.

Tyler'd never been a big believer in prayer, even though his mother had been. He'd been more a doer. If you did enough to prepare, if you planned perfectly, things would go the way they were supposed to. Except, obviously, that wasn't always the way things worked out.

Who knew? He was trying hard not to be resentful of the way life had turned out for him. But when he looked across the street and thought about Sergeant Lane and the pain he must be going through, or when he thought about his brother Ethan and the loss of his family, he figured he had it pretty good.

He had his life. He had people he cared about around him. And options.

God, please let my little brother live to have options, even ones as simple as what to have for dinner.

The hostage taker's voice choked up on the monitor, bringing Tyler back to the room. "Yeah, I promised them a puppy. But I also promised them we'd be a family when I came home."

"Daniel, sometimes when things change, it's so hard to figure out what to do," Gracie said.

"But I can help you figure it out. You have to trust me. You have to put the weapons down and come out."

"I want to see my wife."

Gracie turned around to look at Alisha, who, after a second's hesitation, nodded.

"Alisha's right here, Daniel. She's worried about you and the girls. She wants to make sure you're all okay. But you have to put the weapon down and come out."

"I want to see you first. I want to look you in the face and see if you're telling the truth."

Tyler's mouth went dry. Gracie shot a look at Cruse Conyers, who shook his head. *No.*

She punched a button to mute the phone, talked fast. "He's de-escalating. I'll step out on the porch and right back inside the house. This may be the only way to get him out of the house, Cruse."

Tight-lipped with displeasure, Cruse gave a short nod.

"Give me just a minute, Daniel. It's against the rules, but I'll try to make it happen."

Within seconds of hanging up the phone, she was wired for the recorder and in body armor. Tyler couldn't quite make sense of it, the pretty, smart psychologist who wore rainbow shirts and this warrior in battle armor.

She nodded at Cruse and made the call back to the house. "I'm ready to come out on the porch, Daniel, but you have to do something for me first. You have to let me talk to Matt. I need to know that he's okay."

For long seconds, they only heard shuffling and knocking, but then Matt's voice came over the line. "Hey guys."

Tyler let out a breath he hadn't know he'd been holding. Matt was alive.

"Matt, it's Gracie VanDoren. Are you hurt?"

"No. The girls are fine, too. Scared, but they're not hurt." Tyler could hear the strain in Matt's voice.

Daniel Lane's voice came over the line. "All right, I did what you want. Now you do what I want. Come out where I can see you."

Tyler knew that if Daniel was coming to the window or door to take a look at Gracie, the snipers would most likely have a lethal solution to this standoff. It wouldn't be their first choice, but ultimately, getting everyone out alive was the team's goal.

"Daniel, let's talk about this for a second. You want to see Alisha. She's agreed. You want to see me first. And you've shown good faith by letting me talk to Matt, so I'm going to step out on the porch. You'll see me standing behind two officers. They're only there to protect me."

As she walked out, two of the officers on the Crisis Response Team in full gear stepped in front of her. Holding their shields, they were a formidable barrier. She could be seen from across the street, but she didn't make herself a target.

She was playing it smart. Tyler released another pent-up breath, the tension around him in the small living room palpable.

"All right, Daniel. Can you see me?" Gracie's voice was audible on the speaker, and through the open door he could see her bright hair, gleaming in the late afternoon sun.

"Yes." The hostage taker peered through a crack in the door across the street.

"I did what you asked. Now it's your turn again, Daniel." Gracie's voice, smooth and calm, came through the speaker, and Tyler knew that Daniel Lane was hearing the same thing.

"You want me to put the gun down and come out there. And you're going to let me see my wife?"

Gracie nodded, blond curls bouncing.

"That's the deal. You put the gun down and come out, you get to see her. Everybody wins."

"Okay."

The word, simply delivered, electrified the room.

Gracie looked through the door into the room where they waited. "You got that, Captain?"

"Got it." Cruse spoke into his headset, telling the team to stand by for surrender.

The remainder of the Crisis Response Team, what effectively was a multi-agency SWAT team, moved into position, their weapons raised, ready to arrest Daniel Lane when he came through the door.

Silently, those in the room across the street watched the door of the duplex. The door cracked open and a man stepped out into the light with his hands in the air, squinting in the late afternoon sun.

SIX

Gracie switched to the megaphone that one of the officers handed her. "Daniel, this is Gracie. Please, put the gun on the ground. Very slowly."

Wearing khaki shorts and a T-shirt, he looked like any other military man home for the day, ready to mow the yard or play with the kids. As he laid the gun on the ground, the street erupted in sound, the CRT yelling for him to get on the ground with his hands behind his head. The first to get to him kicked the gun away and, just like that, it was over.

Gracie walked back into the room and laid her headset down, resting both her hands on the table and letting her head drop. She took one long, deep breath. Her legs felt like cooked spaghetti. She wasn't sure they would hold her up.

"Gracie, look." At Tyler's command, she

lifted her head. Through the window, she caught sight of the two little girls, Tabitha and Shandy, as they broke free from the cop holding their hands and took off across the street toward their mother. Alisha dropped to her knees and was nearly bowled over as they barreled into her.

Tyler's heavy hand dropped onto her shoulder and squeezed as his brother Matt stepped onto the porch, squinting at the commotion, rubbing one hand over his short, dark hair. A shout came from the cordoned area as his fiancée, Lara, broke through the barrier.

When Matt reached the bottom of the stairs, Lara leaped. He caught her, his arms clutching her close to his chest, lips moving as he murmured into her ear.

Gracie unstrapped the bullet-resistant vest and dropped it into the chair she'd been sitting in, exhaustion overwhelming her now that the adrenaline was fading.

"You did good, Doc." Tyler sat on the edge of the homeowner's table so he could face her. "Are you finished here, ready for a ride home?"

"You have no idea how ready I am." She slung her purse over her shoulder. "There will be paperwork galore, but I need to get out of here."

He walked beside her to the door, then shot her a sidelong glance. "You have to eat, right?"

"Yes." She drew the word out, wondering what he was getting at.

"Good. Me, too."

"Tyler, I'm exhausted. I'm sweaty. I have a mountain of paperwork to do from this. I really don't think I'd be very good company." Gracie looked up at him and the excuses trailed off. He was smiling, but there was a hint of vulnerability in his expression.

She sighed. How could she say no? She would be thinking of that moment for days—the look on his face when he caught single mother Alisha Lane as she collapsed. His head bowed toward Alisha as he prayed for her children.

Gracie's eyes teared up. She needed to decompress. But did she want to decompress with Tyler?

"I have to drive you to your car anyway."

"Fine." She laughed. "Are all the Clark men as stubborn as you are?"

"Yep. We're a bundle of joy."

They passed the squad car where Daniel

Lane had been cuffed and put in the backseat. His former wife, Alisha, was sitting in the front. She'd followed through on her promise.

He glanced up at Gracie as she walked past. He obviously recognized her. No smile. But he nodded. Maybe it was *Thanks*, maybe it was *I can't believe you robbed me of the one thing I really wanted.* It didn't really matter. Everyone got out safely. It was a win for Gracie and her team.

Lost in thought, Gracie leaned against the side of the truck while Tyler unlocked the door.

He opened the door for her, holding her hand as she climbed in. As he stepped in on his side, he punched numbers into his cell phone. "I need to call my mom. She's only just now gotten used to having us all where she can keep an eye on us and if she heard— well, do you mind?"

"Please call her." Gracie stared out the window at the house where all the drama had taken place. It didn't look like the kind of place where an armed man would hold two little girls hostage. A man who'd been pushed to his breaking point. What did it take to get there?

How much loss could one person stand?

"Yes, ma'am. He's fine. And the girls are doing good, too. Gracie talked the guy into putting his gun down and surrendering. She was awesome. You should've heard her."

Gracie could hear Tyler's mom talking but not what she was saying. Her cell phone beeped and she dug through her purse to find it. As Tyler said goodbye to his mom, she thumbed the button to pop up her text messages.

YOU WON'T BE AS LUCKY AS THOSE LITTLE GIRLS.

She slammed the phone shut.

"Gracie, what is it?"

Instead of answering, she opened the phone and showed him the message. "It's probably nothing, right?"

He didn't answer. "Is there a number?"

"Blocked." She stared out the window. This was beyond anything she'd experienced before. No one had tried to get to her through her cell phone before.

"Okay, listen, let's get some food in you and then we'll go through the files and see if we can make a list of who might have something to gain by hurting you."

She sighed. "I'm not sure I'll be very good company."

"My mom is worried about us. She'd planned a family dinner. I thought we'd skip it, but she wants to go ahead with it." He sent her an apologetic look. "She'd really love to take care of you after what happened today."

"Like I said...I probably won't be good company."

"You don't have to be good company. Marcus will be there. I have to warn you though, my mom's a terrible cook."

Despite everything, Gracie had to laugh at Tyler's pained expression. "And you invited me for dinner?"

"Don't worry, she almost always orders in when we're all coming over."

"I'm going to tell her you said that," she teased.

Tyler turned the corner into an older residential neighborhood, one that even in their beach community had large trees and that stand-the-test-of-time look about it. He pulled into the driveway of a long ranch house and parked, shooting a sideways look at her. "You go ahead and tell her whatever you want. I'm her favorite."

Gracie slid out of the truck and straightened

her skirt as her feet hit the ground. She leaned back into the truck. "Tyler, don't you know mothers tell all their kids that? She probably told Matt and Marcus they're her favorites, too."

The smile dropped into a scowl.

She was chuckling as she walked toward the front door, which was thrown open as she climbed the first step.

Marcus stood in the space, his shorts around his hips, sporting a Sea Breeze Middle School shirt with a big grass stain running down the side. "'Bout time you got here. I'm starving. Where's Matt and Lara?"

Tyler pushed past the kid, who already acted like a brother, gripping Gracie by the hand and pulling her along behind him. "I'm not sure they're coming. It's been a crazy afternoon."

Marcus dropped his head back and let out a groan. "I'm not gonna make it."

"Stop bellyaching, Marcus. Now go put your belt back on so we don't have to look at your boxer shorts during dinner." Matt's mother, a small powerhouse of a woman, reached for Gracie's hand. "I'm Bethanne. You must be Gracie. It's so nice to meet you."

Bethanne was impeccably dressed in a

business suit, but bare toes tipped with deep lavender polish dug into the thick carpet.

"I'm going to make sure the squirt puts on his belt." Tyler started down the hall after Marcus. As they walked down the hall, Tyler leaned toward the teenager and Gracie heard him ask, "Hey, has Mom ever told you she likes you best?"

Marcus threw his arm around Tyler. "Dude, I hate to break it to you, but she does like me best."

Gracie laughed as Tyler gave Marcus a half-hearted shove.

Bethanne Clark turned to Gracie. "Is there something I should know?"

"Tyler told me he's your favorite."

"He is. They all are. It depends on what day of the week it is." Tyler's mother shed her suit coat and tossed it on one of the chairs in the family room.

"That's what I told him. He didn't take it well."

Bethanne snorted an unladylike laugh and put her arm around Gracie. "I think we're going to be good friends. Sweet tea?"

"You have no idea how good that would be right now."

"I think I might. We owe you quite a debt.

Reed is at a sheriff's meeting out of town, but we are both so, so grateful that Matthew is safe."

A flush started in the middle of Gracie's chest. She could feel the heat creeping toward her face. "I was just doing my job."

Bethanne laughed. "That's just what Matt would say."

"What's just what Matt would say?" Matt's dark head poked through the door into the entrance hall.

"Nothing, you rascal. Now get in here and let me see you." Tyler's mom threw her arms around her son.

Matt allowed his mother to look him over, rolling his eyes when she tsk'd over a bruise on his cheekbone. Finally, he grabbed her hands. "Mom, I'm fine."

Matt's fiancée, Lara, a sturdy blonde in jeans and a ponytail, pushed into the room. "He's cranky, too. I think we should feed him." She held a hand out to Gracie. "Hi, Doc. I'm Lara. I heard you did an amazing job talking that guy down today."

"I'm glad things turned out the way they did."

Tyler's mom shooed them toward the kitchen as Tyler and Marcus came back into the room.

"I brought home barbecue for dinner—Matt's favorite. And Tyler made dessert earlier today. Right?"

"Yes, ma'am. It's already in the refrigerator."

Gracie loved the way Tyler spoke to his mom. There was gentle teasing, but she could tell that he loved and respected her.

"Marcus, bring everyone some tea, please. I set the kitchen table."

Bethanne lit fat candles as a centerpiece as they gathered around the table. After putting the matches away, she paused beside Gracie and reached for her hand.

Gracie looked down at their joined fingers. Small and strong, the hand gripped hers. She felt Tyler move to her side and take her other hand.

Bethanne cleared her throat. "We have a lot to be thankful for. Matt is home, all in one piece. We're here around my kitchen table, and Gracie has joined us."

"Tyler, bless the food for us."

Beside her, Gracie felt Tyler go still. But he began to pray and his deep voice, as he thanked God for his brother's safety, went husky.

Gracie heard Bethanne, beside her, sniff.

She had to blink a few times to clear the moisture from her own eyes.

She didn't know Tyler very well, but she did know this: Whatever he thought about the things he had done in the past, he was trying hard to be a good man when it counted. She had to tread carefully here. When her father died, so did her last close tie with family. Being here with Tyler's family felt natural. It was an easy fit.

She knew, as a psychologist, that she could so easily let her own need for connection make her feel things for Tyler that weren't there.

Gracie glanced at him from underneath her eyelashes. His jaw bunched as he fought for control. She gave his hand a gentle squeeze and thought again, *Yeah, very carefully.*

"Amen." Tyler held to Gracie's fingers like a lifeline as Marcus dove for the plate of ribs.

Behind them, she heard her cell phone beep in her purse. She froze for a second, then stood. "Excuse me. It's probably Cruse wondering why I haven't filed my report yet. I don't think the man ever sleeps."

Bethanne Clark smiled. "When that baby of his arrives, he's going to find out what real sleepless nights are like."

With fumbling fingers, Gracie found her

phone and punched the button. *New Multi-media MSG* appeared in the screen. *Receive message?*

Oh, there was a choice? Then she'd go with no.

"What is it, Doc?" Tyler spoke over her shoulder.

"I'm scared to press the button. Crazy, huh?" Annoyed at herself, she pressed OK.

"Someone is getting a kick out of sending threatening messages. But the last time she got one is the night she found her dad's house filled with gas." Tyler shot Matt a pointed look, which Gracie didn't miss.

Bethanne Clark apparently didn't miss it either. "Are you helping Gracie find whoever this person is, Tyler?"

Tyler looked at Gracie and raised an eyebrow.

"I didn't think there was any need to make a big deal out of it. I get hate mail all the time. But," she said as Tyler's face grew darker, "this feels different." Her stomach churned as she saw the picture. The inside of her house, where she lived. She flipped the phone around so he could see the picture.

"This *is* different," Tyler said. "Whether it's

an attempt to hurt you or just scare you, this person is systematically stalking you."

Gracie opened her mouth to retort, but Beth-anne spoke before she could. "Gracie, do you have a roommate?"

Gracie shook her head.

"A big dog?"

"Just a slightly overweight cat, who I really need to get home and check on. I'm sorry. I really don't feel like eating anymore." She looked from Bethanne to Tyler, who seemed to be sharing some sort of silent communication between mother and son.

Tyler nodded as he backed toward the hall. "I was already planning on it. I'll just grab something to wear from here until I can swing by my place tomorrow."

"Do you really think that's necessary?"

Bethanne Clark put her arm around Gracie. "Honey, if there's someone out there who wants to do you harm, it's necessary."

Tyler reappeared, his keys in his hand. "If you're ready, we can go. Unless you want to eat?"

The thought of eating anything made her feel sick. "I think I'd better get home and check things out. Thank you so much for having me,

Bethanne. I hope we can do it again sometime when we're not in crisis mode."

Bethanne folded Gracie into a hug. "Of course we'll do it again, sweetie. Now you let me know if there's anything I can do. And keep that son of mine in line."

"I'll try." Gracie smiled, despite the fact that her heart was breaking. Even though she'd been thirteen when her mom died, there were few real memories when she hadn't been sick. Her mom's perfume, cuddling in the bed in soft-crisp sheets to read stories, a kiss on the forehead.

It had been so long that she didn't even notice missing her mother, but being with Tyler's mom gave her just a glimpse of what it would be like to have someone cherish her. For no other reason than she existed.

Matt stood, too. "Call if you need backup."

"You got it. Listen, for the crème brulée, just take it out of the fridge. I left the blowtorch on the counter. *Lightly* crust the top before eating it, okay?"

"Blowtorch? All right!"

Lara shook her head. "Thanks a lot, Tyler."

"Don't mention it." He held the door open for Gracie.

As she stepped over the threshold into the night, she shivered. Tyler walked beside her toward the truck. Muscular, strong, smart—Tyler could keep her safe. But she was entering uncharted territory.

And she didn't know if even her faith would be enough to get her through.

SEVEN

Tyler glanced at Gracie as they drove through the dark streets of Sea Breeze. Silent, she stared out the window of his truck. With the last text message and the consequent decision for him to stay on her property, it was almost as if she'd shut down.

Give him a character to play, and he knew exactly what to do and what to say. In this situation, as himself, faced with Gracie's silence, he had no clue. "It's been a tough day, huh?"

She didn't answer, just stared out the window at the passing scenery, which wasn't that interesting. Maybe he should just leave her alone.

After several more minutes, she turned to face him. "So we're going to go through the file tonight?"

"Do you want to?" He pulled into the driveway and parked. The security lights around her house, equipped with motion detectors, came on. He reached under the seat for his semiautomatic. "Stay in the truck with the doors locked. Don't get out until I come for you."

She nodded, and in the dim light he could see the tension around her mouth as she held out the key to her house.

Tyler was exposed as he crossed the pool deck to her home. Ten quick soundless steps and he was at the front door, the only noise the shushing and bubbling of the jets as they circulated the water in the pool.

Locked. So how did their perpetrator get in?

He pushed the key into the lock and turned it, still thinking about it. Their perp could've picked it. If the person was good enough, he might not see scratch marks. He could see the kitchen and great room from the front door.

Maybe Gracie left a window open somewhere. He checked the windows in the guest room. Nope. The master bedroom windows were locked, too, and the room was empty. Tyler dropped to look under the bed. His heart nearly jumped out of his chest as a pair of green glowing eyes stared at him. He blew out a breath and tried to make his heart rate return to something resembling normal. "Charlemagne. Here, kitty, kitty."

The cat growled. At least Tyler thought it was a growl. Regardless, that cat wasn't coming out of there.

Climbing to his feet, he tucked the weapon into the waistband of his jeans and dropped his shirttails over it. There were a couple of other possibilities for entry. A professional might make a mold and have a key made. But he or she would've needed access to Gracie's keys at some point.

Mulling over several potential scenarios, Tyler walked back across the pool deck toward the truck. Just because the photo was sent today didn't mean it was taken today. They needed to take a closer look at it to see.

Opening the door for Gracie, he said, "Coast is clear. Come on in, Dr. Sunshine."

"What did you call me?" Gracie swung her bag over her shoulder—the big yellow one, the color of sunshine.

He fought a smile. "You heard me."

As soon as she stepped in the door, the cat trotted out, loudly meowing his discontent.

"He wouldn't come out from under the bed when I called him."

Gracie poured cat food into a dish on the

kitchen floor. "I guess he has discriminating taste."

Tyler clutched his chest. "Ouch. Okay, so you ready to make a pot of coffee and get started on that file?"

"Uh..." She stalled on her way to the kitchen table.

"What?" He got a look at her face. "Oh, no. Don't tell me you don't have coffee."

"Okay, I won't tell you." She smiled, but he could see fatigue in her eyes. "I do have some nice Darjeeling."

"Is that supposed to make me feel better?"

Gracie's smile deepened, the dimple winking just below her lip. He wanted to touch it.

"Tea is good for you. You should try it."

"I'll take your word for it and try it another time." He sat at the table and took half the file that she pulled out of her briefcase. "Let's get this over with. We're most likely looking for a woman. I'd say that ninety-five percent of these letters are from men, maybe more."

She took the other half of the stack of letters. "Maria said the hair she was analyzing was the color of mine, but it had been dyed, so that's not going to help us narrow it down."

"It'll take some legwork and phone calls,

figuring out which of these women are still in jail. Finding out if any of them have family members angry enough to blame you." His eyes briefly touched her face before focusing on the task at hand. "Meanwhile, Maria will be working on the DNA evidence. Maybe it will tell us something."

Tyler flipped the first page over. And then the next.

He whistled. "Boy, you've got some real winners here."

"Yeah, my 'fans' are nothing if not creative." She flipped through her own stack, only separating one woman from the first ten or fifteen letters.

After two hours, they'd gone through the whole file and come up with a list of eight women, three of whom had been released in the past two months. The rest had been out over a year.

Gracie dropped her head and rubbed the place on her neck where the muscles burned. "It's been a really long day and it doesn't seem like we've gotten very far."

Tyler laid his pencil down. "When I joined the DEA, there was a lot of backslapping, take-down-the-bad-guy kind of camaraderie. It's great to some extent—a different kind of family." He looked over at her. "There was this one older guy in my office who'd been around for a while. He had deep rings under his eyes and always looked a little rumpled. I thought at first he was one of those washed-up types. I found out later that he was a closer. They gave him the cases no one else could handle." He paused, as if lost in thought.

"Go on," Gracie said, clearly intrigued.

"Well, late one night, we were doing some background on my first undercover case. I was all gung ho, ready to go out and kick some dirt, find out where the drugs were. This guy told me to slow down and really consider what I was doing, that I shouldn't forget there was a price to being a hero."

She held her chin in her hand. "What did you say?"

"I blew him off...but he was right. I didn't know how right until this last assignment." He wasn't looking at her, instead focusing on neatly stacking the files they'd rejected.

"Were you the one who paid the price?"

He glanced up and smiled, the moment gone. She'd pushed and he took a figurative step away from her. "My point is—and yeah, there really is one—getting everyone out alive today was a major win, but it takes something out of you. I wanted you to know I understand that."

She nodded, her throat aching as she thought of him being undercover and alone, suffering the cost of being a hero with no one to hold him up. She wasn't going to let that happen again.

"Well, we've got a starting place. Tomorrow we'll know more." Tyler stood and stretched his back. "Come on. Walk me to the door and I'll go find a place to sleep in that homey little cabin of forty-two rooms you grew up in."

"Ha, ha." But as she walked to the door, she turned back to him. "I don't deserve how nice you've been to me. Thank you."

He didn't let her even finish her sentence before he started shaking his head. "Nope. It doesn't work that way. You don't get to be grateful. We're friends. Or at least I think we are." Tyler walked toward her, dodging the cat that twined between his legs, head-butting him. "I had some time. My life is not exactly planned out right now."

She picked up the cat, laughing a little as the enormous feline bumped her nose. "I know how that feels. And yes, we're friends, and I'm thankful for it. See you in the morning?"

"You leave for work around seven forty-five?" At her nod, he continued, "Okay, I'll knock on your door. Don't open it unless you see me."

"All right."

He closed the door behind him. She gave him a thumbs up and smiled. He shook his head. Doctor Sunshine. She was terrified and exhausted, but she still managed to smile.

He picked his bag up from the porch and skirted the pool as he made his way toward the big house. Now, to check out that stove.

Gracie flicked off her hair dryer and wrestled it into the drawer, huge diffuser attachment and all. Had she heard something? Surely it wasn't Tyler already.

She picked up her cell phone to check the time. No, it was only seven-fifteen.

Padding down the short hall, she peeked around the corner into the living room. Sure enough, there he was at the door. Well, he wasn't exactly at the door. He was pacing.

She went to open the door and noticed that he looked slightly annoyed. He was also rumpled and had deep circles under his eyes.

"Did I miss something? I thought we said seven forty-five." She leaned against the door frame.

"No, it's just… I was worried when you didn't answer the door."

"I was drying my hair. I couldn't hear you."

"Okay, good." He turned to walk away.

She stared after him as he got nearly to the edge of the pool before she cleared her throat. "Tyler? Was there something you wanted?"

He stopped but didn't turn around. "I made breakfast. You know, if you want some. It's on the patio."

Her chest squeezed tight, tears really close to the surface. Hormones, had to be. Because she wouldn't get all emotional over someone fixing her breakfast. Had it been that long since someone cared enough to take care of her? "Give me just a minute."

She slid her feet into her work shoes and grabbed her briefcase, skidding to a stop right outside the door. One of the pool lounge chairs had been pulled close to the door. A blanket was tossed at the end. She shook her head. One of the forty-two rooms in the house, huh?

Tyler met her on the patio of the main house as he came out the back door with a pot of coffee. "It's really nice out here. The view of the pool looking out over the bay is incredible."

"You should know. You woke up to that view." She gave him the look that Mrs. Batterson used to give her when her behavior was mystifying.

"Oh. That. It wouldn't have been much safer for you if I was in the big house until we get you a security system installed. I have a friend coming to do it, but he can't get here for a day or two. Tea?"

"Yes, please." She sat in the chair, staring at the table.

He'd made chocolate chip pancakes with fresh berries on the side. A linen-lined basket covered some kind of muffin and a beautifully fluffy breakfast quiche sat in the middle of the table on a pedestal with some of the garden flowers around the bottom.

He must've been working in the kitchen since four a.m. "Tyler, I know Mrs. Batterston keeps the kitchen stocked with basics like the coffee and flour, but this—this is not basic."

"I had the berries in the car, left over from what I bought to garnish the dessert last night. Everything else really is just basic."

She sat in the chair he held out for her and slid closer to the table, first biting into the chocolate chip pancakes. "*Tyler.* Really, this is—okay, give me some quiche."

His smile flashed white as he dished it onto a waiting plate. His food was making her very happy, but apparently her enjoyment was good for him, too. The full-on grin from former DEA agent Tyler Clark was a rarity.

"Aren't you going to have some?" She waved to the chair beside her. "Please, sit down. You're going to make me nervous, and I really want to be able to enjoy this."

He poured himself a cup of coffee, black, from the other pot and sat back in his chair. "You know, the La Cornue range you have in the kitchen is unbelievable. It's the best quality I've cooked with."

Gracie stopped with a bite of the quiche halfway to her mouth. "Really? My mom hated that thing. At least from what I can remember. She didn't cook much, though."

Tyler chuckled. "Well, we have that in common. At our house, the microwave was our best friend."

"Mine just couldn't deal with it. Looking back now, with a professional's eyes, I think she was probably clinically depressed." She didn't like thinking about her mom, thinking about what those lonely years would've been like if her mom had reached out for help.

She took another bite of pancakes. Oh, he

was good. "Have you thought about doing something with your cooking skill? You really do have a talent—I think it must be something you're either born with or not."

"I've thought about it, but I don't want to open a restaurant. Maybe catering, but I'm not sure I have the people skills to pull it off since my last 'posse' consisted of a bunch of thugs and drug dealers."

"Sometimes I've thought about turning this place into a bed and breakfast. It seems like a house that should be full of laughter, families and children. I wouldn't know where to begin to do it, though." She shoved another bite of pancakes into her mouth, her eyes nearly rolling back in her head as the melted chocolate exploded on her tongue.

He looked around, a thoughtful look on his face. "You know, you're right. There should be kids cannon balling into the pool. Right now."

She sat for a second, lifted her tea cup and took a sip. The big diesel engine of a tugboat pushing a barge on the bay rumbled. A tender breeze ruffled the cloth he'd put on the table, and the only raucous sound seemed to be the mockingbird in the tree down on the lawn. It seemed pretty perfect right now. "Maybe not right this exact second. As for you, you don't seem to be lacking in people skills to me. But you don't have to make a decision today. You have time." She glanced at her cell phone. "Something I'm out of. Can I catch a ride to the office since my car's still there?"

He went still for a minute, then stood and began gathering dishes. "I've got to drop by my place to get some things anyway. Why don't you get your briefcase while I put breakfast away?"

"Hey, Tyler? Can I take the muffins to work? I always wanted to be the popular kid."

The laugh took her by surprise, and while it sounded a little rusty, it was a beautiful sound. She couldn't help wondering what cost he had borne that had taken his laugh away...

And what would it take to bring it back for good?

Tyler flipped to his back and drifted toward shore, his exhausted muscles not willing to swim another stroke. The temperature in the Gulf, even in April, was still a chilly sixty-five, so he wore a wetsuit to combat hypothermia.

He swam for the same reason he cooked— it was worth the effort just to escape all the thoughts that kept his brain in constant overdrive and to focus on one thing. One stroke after the other.

Some days the Gulf took all his concentration just to stay alive. Other days she tried to trick him into believing she was innocuous, a beautiful crystal-clear lake of emerald green.

His feet touched the sand and he battled for balance, his tired muscles burning at the effort. He'd left his towel on the beach directly in front of the small condo he'd rented for the month. It was still early for the college kids on spring break to be out and about, but a few families had made their way to the sand since he'd hit the water an hour ago. He dodged one toddler in a droopy bathing suit and barely missed being hit in the face with the flying shovel of another.

Gracie had tossed that compliment at him almost as an afterthought. For her, maybe it was. It had completely flummoxed him. Was it possible that it wasn't just criminals that he had a way with? Maybe he'd been the one feeling out of place and no one else had really noticed.

Picking up his towel, he rubbed the salt water out of his hair as he trudged toward his condo. He climbed the short steps to his porch and found his brother sitting on his porch drinking a cup of coffee.

"Glad to see you made yourself at home." Tyler unzipped his wetsuit and left it hanging, pulling a dry T-shirt over his head from the pile collecting on the table.

Matt shrugged. "You have better coffee than I do."

"Agreed." Tyler's calves were cramping up. He leaned against the wall and placed his heel flat on the deck floor, making a face as the muscle pulled taut.

"I don't understand why you insist on punishing yourself."

"I don't know what you're talking about. I exercise." Finishing the leg stretch, Tyler looped one arm and then the other in a big, loose circle.

"You do know what I'm talking about. You push yourself to the point of pain and then push a little harder." Matt looked into his coffee. "Are the memories that bad?"

Talking about feelings wasn't really something they did in their family of boys unless their mom made them. Being undercover for years hadn't helped that tendency. Tyler had gotten used to suppressing his own emotions and projecting the feelings of the person he'd had to become.

But he'd come home to find the person he *wanted* to be—not the person he used to be. Maybe talking would help him move past what he saw as a huge boulder in his way. He lifted one shoulder and turned it into a stretch. "I don't know, Matt. You know better than most that I've done things I'm not proud of."

"Fortunately, the things we do in the past don't determine the person that we are in the future. God has a plan for you, Tyler."

Tyler poured coffee into an empty cup and took a sip. Matt was right. He did have good coffee. "You sound like Mom. And I'll tell you what I told her. It would be nice if God would share that plan with me."

"It's not like the 'As Seen on TV' ads for house plans, dude. You can't send in two hundred and ninety-nine dollars and get a set of plans for you and one for the builder. It doesn't work that way." He walked to the edge of the deck and leaned on the rail. "But if you're praying for direction, God will give it. I do feel compelled to warn you, though. Sometimes God provides answers in completely unexpected ways."

Tyler shook his head, even as he thought

about Gracie and her idea for a B&B. "It all feels awkward, you know? Every relationship. I've been away so long."

"Well, you're back now. I hope you stay. And I actually didn't come by just to drink your coffee."

Tyler smirked. "Did you come by to raid my stash of Twizzlers?"

"No, although now that I know you've laid in a supply of Twizzlers, I'll be by for those. I wanted to ask you to be my best man."

He was caught off guard by the request. "You're sure you want me?"

"I asked, didn't I?"

Tyler nodded, a big lump in his throat that he didn't trust himself to talk around. He held out a hand and Matt slammed it with his, looping his arm around Tyler's neck for a back-slapping hug.

"Great. Now Lara can get off my back about it." Matt laughed. "Get measured for a tux. Okay? She gave me a list seven pages long of stuff to do, so I better get going. Love ya, man."

"You too, bro." Leaving the DEA had been hard. His identity had been tied up in being an undercover cop. He wanted to believe God had a plan for his life, that all the things he'd been through, all the things he'd seen and done, could be brought together and made to work in some weird way.

He just couldn't see it. But maybe God could.

It was lunch hour by the time Gracie made her way back to her office from appointments at the county jail. She whipped into a parking place in front of Sip This. Her favorite coffee shop had the best ham sandwiches made with homemade bread.

She placed her order with the cashier, Julie, and handed over her debit card. In a few seconds, Julie came back with the card and a strange expression on her face. "I'm really sorry, Doc. Your card wouldn't go through."

Gracie felt her face flush. It had to be a mistake because she'd just put her paycheck in a couple of days ago. "Do you mind trying it again? There's really no reason for it to be declined."

Julie pressed her lips together. "I tried it three times. I'm sorry."

"Why don't we let lunch be on me?" a voice said at her shoulder. Gracie looked around to see an impeccably dressed Bethanne Clark, looking every inch the hospital administrator today. Now she really wanted to sink into the floor.

"It's really not necessary, Bethanne. I'll stop by the bank on my way back to work. I'm sure it's just a mistake."

"Well, you may as well figure it out on a full stomach. I'll have the veggie stack and a mango tea to go with whatever Gracie's having, Julie."

With a bakery bag holding their sandwiches, Bethanne led the way to a courtyard table. She sank into a chair and sighed, dropping her laptop case to the ground beside her. "Peace at last."

"That bad, huh?"

"I'm taking a break from my office. I can't work for five minutes without someone interrupting me, so I thought lunch on the terrace here sounded heavenly. Won't you join me?" Bethanne waved a hand at the chair next to her.

With a fleeting thought to the work piled up on her own desk at work, Gracie pulled out the chair opposite Bethanne and smiled. The woman had just paid for Gracie's lunch. If she wanted company, she got company. "Maybe you should make this the hospital annex."

"No, then everyone would know where to

bother me. I think we should keep it our little secret. Speaking of secrets, I don't guess it is one, but Matthew told me that you don't date. Is it for religious reasons or personal ones? I ask because I think my Tyler has his eye on you." She tilted her head and smiled. "I could just keep my nose in my own business, but what fun would that be?"

Gracie stopped with her ham sandwich halfway to her lips. "I don't have any ethical or moral problem with people dating, in general." She pulled the chain out from under her clothes and showed Bethanne the charm. "My mom and dad gave me this purity ring when I was thirteen. I remember thinking my father was a little off his rocker when he started talking about not dating but instead just being friends with boys and waiting to find the person who is my best friend and soul mate."

"That seems so logical when you think about it." Bethanne's eyes, the color of sweet dark chocolate, and the exact image of Tyler's, were kind.

"It's true that I can tell a lot more about a guy when we're friends than I could if we were dating. Like I watched how Tyler treated you at dinner the other night. It's clear that he cherishes you and really respects you."

"Interesting observation. Do you think that would predict how he would treat a wife?"

"In theory." She smiled at Bethanne. "In reality, I've learned people don't always act the way they're supposed to."

The leaves of the oak tree in the courtyard had just started to bud and made a breathtaking green canopy above them, swaying in the breeze from the ocean across the street.

"It sounds like you have a good head on your shoulders, Gracie. Did you and Tyler manage to make any progress in your case last night?"

"Some. Tyler's really been a Godsend to me. I guess you know that." She took a bite of her sandwich, but she wasn't really hungry.

Bethanne picked at the veggies on hers. "He's always been one to jump into the fray, trying to make a difference. I shouldn't have underestimated him when he was away."

"I think Tyler is very good at putting other people's well-being ahead of his own, even if it came to keeping you safe by letting you believe something about him that wasn't true."

Quick tears came to Bethanne's eyes. "Very

astute of you. Now, I have a one o'clock meeting or I would be happy to sit here and chat under the oak trees with you all afternoon. Another time?"

"Of course."

As Bethanne picked up her portfolio case and darted toward her car, Gracie fought the cold feeling in the pit of her stomach. It had been lucky running into Bethanne, or she would've been without lunch.

Did the person threatening her have the reach to get to her bank accounts?

Gracie shivered despite the warm spring sunshine. How much was this person capable of? And how far would he or she go?

EIGHT

Tyler was waiting for Gracie outside the police department. He pushed away from the wall as she came through the front doors. "Hey there, you ready for your taxi ride home?"

"Do you think you could just follow me home? I feel weird leaving my car here." Her voice was muted, the usual quiet confidence missing.

"Sure." Tyler didn't ask any questions, but he put a hand on her back, just to let her know she wasn't alone. He wondered as he followed her home: Where was the woman who'd drawn a smiley face on the marker board on her door, the first day he'd met her?

He made the turn into Gracie's driveway and parked behind her. She got out first and made a beeline toward her house. "Gracie."

She stopped but didn't turn around. "What?"

Her voice was clogged with tears. His chest squeezed as he walked up behind her. "I need to go in first, hon. It won't take but a minute, and I promise I'll give you some space. Okay?"

She nodded.

As quickly as he could, he cleared the areas of her house. The rooms smelled vaguely like summer. Like Gracie.

He stepped over the threshold onto the porch. "All clear. Is there anything you need?"

"No thanks. I think I'm just going to eat a bowl of cereal and go to bed. It's been a day."

Her face was splotchy, her lashes spiky with tears. He reached out to tuck a piece of hair behind her ear. "What happened, Gracie?"

"It's just…been a day."

"Want to talk about it?"

She shook her head, her lips tight.

"Okay." He started to turn away but words began to pour out of her.

"I can handle really bad people, you know? And the ones who are genuinely certifiable? I can handle them, too." She swallowed hard. "But the ones who find themselves in an absolutely horrible situation where they don't see a way out except to do something that they would never, ever have considered—those are the ones that tear me up."

"You had one of those cases today?" He eased her toward one of the chairs on the pool deck.

She dropped into the chair and propped up her feet. "A seventeen-year-old boy. I'll recommend that he be tried as a juvenile, but I don't know if they'll go for it. They rarely do these days. Plus, this boy works to support his family because they live with the grandmother. It's such a waste."

"Can you to talk about it? Without giving me any details?" He wanted to hold her hand, wanted to make things right in her world. He was a doer, but maybe in this case, listening was the best thing he could do. He sat facing her in the chair next to hers, leaving his feet on the ground.

"This kid takes care of his little brother, makes sure the boy makes the bus, does his homework, has enough to eat. The grandmother that they live with just got diagnosed with heart disease, but doesn't have insurance, so she can't afford her medication. He can't pay the hospital bills when he's working a minimum-wage job." She sighed heavily. "He robbed a pharmacy. The only thing he took was the medicine that his grandmother needed. He didn't take any other kind of drug, even though there are plenty he could've sold on the street to make some fast cash."

"That poor kid." The breeze off the water blew that curl in front of her face and he tucked it behind her ear again, tilting his head so he could see her face.

"He didn't hurt anyone, but he robbed the store with a gun. It's going to go badly for him, when really what he needed was help. The system is broken, Tyler. Sometimes I just want to run away, but it's all we've got to work with."

"And if you don't stay and fight for the cases like this one, what will happen to them?" He picked a piece of grass off the ground and threw it in the pool.

"Nailed it in one." She looked at him through watery eyes. "Sometimes I'm the only one on their side."

"Want some hot chocolate? I think I saw some chocolate in the pantry supplies, and I bought some milk at the grocery store today."

"Another time, maybe. I'm sorry. This on top of the thing with my bank account was just too much." Gracie smiled at him, despite the fact that her eyes were still full of tears.

"Wait. What happened to your bank account?" His voice was hard and he gentled it with some effort. "Does this have something to do with the threats against you?"

She shrugged, the motion tight with tension. "I guess. Someone apparently took all the money out of my account. The manager said that according to their records I cashed out the account and closed it. Which, of course, I didn't do. The bank is looking into it."

Tyler didn't move. He sat beside her, willing to be there for her while she wanted him to be. It was a far cry from the life he'd been living, a life on the edge, where the edge was the difference between staying alive and ending up dead.

He wanted to care about something bigger than what he was going to do tomorrow, or next week, or next year. Because no matter how big that seemed to him, it wasn't as huge as losing your only family, like that kid faced. But that kid had Gracie on his side.

Anger infused him as he thought about someone systematically stalking her and trying to ruin her. He wasn't going to let that happen. "Tomorrow I'll go to the bank and get a look at the security tapes. We're going to get to the bottom of this, Gracie."

"I know. Listen, I think I'm going to go in. I need to feed Charlemagne."

Tyler watched as she walked toward the house, her skirt swishing. He'd been thinking he was so unlucky to have things happen the way they had with his career, but maybe he was lucky after all, to have met her at the exact moment that he needed to.

At the exact moment she needed him.

He could see her through the window, dropping her purse on the couch. She waved as she turned toward the bedroom.

Maybe he should go up to the main house. He could make that hot chocolate. As good as that sounded, it didn't beat sitting out here in the spring cool air with the audible backdrop of the bay lapping against the sand.

"Tyler!"

The scream came from inside Gracie's house. He reached for his weapon before he remembered that he didn't carry one as a part of his wardrobe anymore. He ran for the door and slammed it open with his shoulder.

"Gracie! Where are you?"

She appeared in the doorway of her bedroom, her eyes wide and frightened. As she came closer, he could see that she wasn't just afraid, she was frantic. Her chest heaved as she tried to take in air.

"What's going on?" he asked urgently.

"It's—Charlemagne." She was totally freaking out, not breathing. "He was here when I left this morning, and he's gone."

Now that she mentioned it, the cat hadn't been trying to trip him as he cleared the house earlier.

"I'm sorry, Tyler, it's just—"

"You don't have to explain. I get it. Did you check the closets?"

"Yes. He's not trapped anywhere. Do you think that woman took him? Oh, Tyler, do you think she did something to Charlemagne?"

"Is his food here?"

Gracie's eyes lit with comprehension and she ran for the kitchen. "No, it's not here. That's good, right? If she took his food, she's planning on keeping him alive."

"Right. She wouldn't have taken the food if she wasn't going to need it." He said the words, and it might even have been true, but he was worried. The fact that the woman had taken something precious to Gracie was worrying, to say the least. On top of all that, she'd also messed with Gracie's finances. All this suggested that the stakes were definitely climbing.

And Gracie looked much too fragile for his liking. As positive as she'd been from the beginning, even her natural optimism was flagging.

"I need to go, Gracie. And you need to get some rest, if you can." He stood and walked toward the door. "We won't stop looking until we know what happened, okay?"

She went still. "You're used to doing that, aren't you?"

"I don't know what you're talking about."

"Being careful with your words. Not telling a lie, but not telling the truth either."

What could he say? It had been so long since he'd been transparent, he didn't even know if he knew how to be anymore. He looked at her, making the effort to let her see his heart in his eyes. "I don't know what I do or don't do, Gracie. Maybe the undercover thing affects what I say. But the truth is I don't want to give you false hope. What you should know is that I won't give up."

Her lip trembled and she swiped at her eyes again. "I'm such a mess. I know he's just a cat, but since my dad died, it's just been me and Charlemagne, and I love that silly cat."

He held her loosely in his arms, just enough so that she would know that he was there, holding her up if she were to fall. "You've had a rough couple of days. Get some sleep and we'll work out what to do tomorrow."

She drew a deep breath. "Okay, you're right. I need rest and a better perspective in the morning."

"I'll wait until you lock up. Tomorrow we'll have the alarm installed." Aware that it was little comfort since her cat had been stolen today, he started for the door and then turned back, unwilling to leave her alone. "Are you sure you're all right? We can get a female officer to come and stay in the house with you."

"I'll be fine."

He wished that her voice held a little more confidence and a little less bravado. And he had to stop himself from pushing the door open again and pulling her into his arms. Instead he took one careful step onto the porch.

With a little wave good-night, Gracie closed the door behind him. According to her, she'd been alone since her dad died, no family except for that bossy cat. And now someone wanted to hurt her. Had hurt her, by taking something precious to her. That much was obvious.

What was equally obvious to him was that she was growing to be more and more important to him. There was no doubt in his mind that he was more than willing to stand between her and harm.

If she'd let him.

The next morning, Gracie opened her front door to find Tyler having coffee on the patio with another man. He stood when he saw her. "Gracie, meet Nolan Ross. He's going to be working on the security system in your place today. We've run down some info on those names we pulled out. You and I are left with the legwork now, so if you can spare a couple of hours this morning we can look into it while Nolan works here."

The security expert, a tall, lanky guy in black motorcycle boots and jeans, nodded to Gracie, barely meeting her eyes. His bed-head hair, which stuck up in random black tufts, looked like he cut it himself. "See you in a few."

Tyler poured hot water into a tea cup and pushed it across the patio table to her as Nolan let himself into her house. "Here's your tea. Did you manage to sleep?"

"He's the best?"

Amusement played around the corner of Tyler's mouth. "I wouldn't have him work on your place if he wasn't."

She flicked her eyes up at him. "He doesn't say much."

"That's because his brain is too full of stuff nobody else understands. Okay, let's take a look at these files. Nolan helped me compile the information last night."

Tyler pulled the eight threatening letters they'd identified. All eight had been released from prison since Gracie testified, three in the past two months. "So yesterday, I started with the furthest date of release to see if I could find out where these women are now. These two—" he pulled two out of the stack of letters, which now had photos attached "—are already back in prison. This one is living in Arkansas with her aunt and, according to her parole officer, is the picture of rehabilitation."

"So, we're down to five." Gracie sipped at her tea and thought, in a slightly dazed way, about the turn her life had taken—to one minute be doing her job, going about her life in the most normal possible way, and in the space of time it took to open an envelope, have everything change. Now she had a disreputable-looking genius installing a security system in her house and an ex-DEA agent pouring her tea and talking about leads.

A really handsome ex-DEA agent. Who happened to be a really good cook.

"You there?" Tyler had moved on to the next group of files.

The list, Gracie. She rubbed a hand through her hair, not caring that she was leaving it a frizzy mess. "Yes, I'm listening. Who's next?"

Tyler pulled two more pages from the stack. "These two are deceased. This one was drugs. The other was labeled as domestic, but the investigating officer I talked to last night said drugs were involved in that one, too."

"That's really sad. Also typical, which to me makes it even more sad." She set her cup down with a clank on the iron patio table.

"This one," he tapped with a thoughtful finger, "is a possibility." He tapped the pages of the remaining two. "These two are maybes, but this one is married and just had a baby last week. This one is working a steady job. I don't think our girl could manage working and stalking you. And I can't picture your stalker with a newborn."

"So it's this one. Shay Smith," she said.

"Maybe. Don't go getting your hopes up about this, Gracie. Nothing's a sure thing."

She pulled the sheet closer, not sure she even remembered the case. A closer look at the photo jogged her memory. Bar fight. Assault and battery. Attempted murder. Later, when one of the victims died, the prosecutors bumped the charges to murder, but it didn't stick.

"I do remember this case. This woman, girl really, tried to sell me on the fact that she lost her temper so completely that she had to be crazy. I wonder if she still has that temper or if she was able to learn how to control it while she was in prison."

"We're about to figure that out. Wonder-geek got us an address last night. She still lives in the area." Tyler gathered up the papers with Shay Smith's on the top and held out a hand to Gracie. "You ready for this?"

She looked at his long, strong fingers. He placed her hand in his, the touch alone giving her the sense of a deeper connection. Her eyes drifted up to meet his and his fingers tightened around hers.

"I'm ready. Ready to find some answers

and find my cat." Gracie had the feeling those
answers—and her cat—weren't going to be so
easy to come by.

Tyler pulled his truck to the side of the road
across from a beat-down house in a neighborhood that might've been nice. Once.

He set the brake and realized Gracie was
clutching the door handle with a white-knuck-
le grip.

"Hey, Doc, you don't have to go in. I can
handle this one." He brushed the fingers of her
other hand with his, not sure just how far he
should go. He wanted to respect her boundar-
ies. And holding her hand earlier, he hadn't
wanted to let go.

She chewed her lip. "I want to talk to her. It's
just, I usually interview people when they're
on their way to trial. We're going to be knocking on the door of a woman with anger issues
who hated me enough to send a letter from
prison telling me all the painful things she'd
like to do to me. It's a little disconcerting."

Disconcerting. That was one word for it.

She stared at the house.

He leaned closer. "Did you notice the
pansies?"

"What?" She didn't know whether to look

at the house or at him, so he pointed to the front porch steps.

"Do mean, hateful people plant pansies?" He shrugged. "I don't think so. Maybe she changed in prison. Grew up."

"Grew a conscience?" She rolled her eyes and drew in a deep breath. "You think I'm being silly?"

He shook his head and this time locked his pointer finger with hers. "No, I think your feelings are justified."

She pushed the unlock button with her other hand and said, "Let's go before I change my mind."

He went around to meet her, slamming the door behind her and beeping the alarm. "It's going to be fine. We'll ask for her, then ask a few questions. That's all."

At the door, Gracie seemed to shake off her nervousness and knocked. A few minutes later, a woman answered the door. Tall and thin with dark brown hair pulled back into a ponytail, Shay Smith was wearing jeans and a plain white V-neck T-shirt. She looked about fourteen, instead of the twenty-eight that she now was.

"Hi, I'm Dr.—"

"I know who you are." The woman

interrupted before Gracie could get two words out. Tyler stepped up and lounged against the wall next to Gracie.

The woman's eyes shot to him and then back to Gracie. "What do you want?"

Gracie smoothed her skirt and folded her hands. "We'd really just like to speak with you. Ask a few questions, that's all."

"What about?" Although she wasn't exactly friendly, she looked more nervous than anything. Her dark brown hair, unlike the fake blond sample found in Gracie's home, was one mark in Shay Smith's favor.

"May we come in?" Tyler inserted the question before Gracie could answer.

Shay dodged to the other side of the door, more fearful of him than Gracie. Apparently, he still had cop presence.

She opened the door wider and Gracie walked in. He followed a little more slowly, wanting to see if anything looked out of place. Or maybe he would see a gigantic orange-and-white tabby that didn't look like it belonged.

The house had definitely seen better days. There were empty glasses on the end table, a newspaper scattered on the coffee table, but there were small touches, like the pansies, everywhere. A framed magazine picture on the wall, a lit candle on the table. Someone cared about this place. He had a feeling it was Shay Smith.

Gracie had jumped into the conversation with her usual leading questions, trying to get Shay to open up. So far she seemed to be doing pretty well. The woman, who had spent six years behind bars, had tears in her eyes.

"I can't believe you came here. I thought a lot about what I said to you—how I wrote that letter. I was real angry when I said those things to you, Dr. VanDoren. I didn't mean what I said. I'm sorry."

Gracie smiled. "I think you might've meant it at the time. But I understand."

"I got clean in jail. If it hadn't been for jail, I'd probably be dead by now." She rubbed damp eyes with her finger and thumb. "In a way, it was the best thing that ever happened to me."

Gracie had become the good cop, the one that Shay identified with. He could be the bad cop. It fit him like a second skin. "Where were you yesterday afternoon?"

"Right here. I'm always right here." Shay lifted her jeans leg. An electronic monitoring device circled her ankle. "It was a condition of my release. I can't leave my property."

She shrugged narrow shoulders. "I couldn't have done whatever it is you're thinking I might've."

Gracie shot a hard look at Tyler. So he was the bad cop in her eyes, too. "No one is accusing you of anything. We had a list of people who wrote letters to me who've since been released, that's all. You're doing great, Shay. Keep it up."

Shay walked them to the door. Gracie hugged her, while Tyler jingled his keys on the porch and kept watch down the street.

"When you get ready to find a job, get in touch with me at the police station. I have some friends who might be looking for someone who has a way with flowers," Gracie said as she backed toward him.

"You're really a nice lady, Dr. VanDoren. I'm glad I got to see you again."

"Take care of yourself, Shay. You've put the old life behind you. Make sure it stays there."

"I will, thanks."

Tyler held the truck door open for Gracie to climb in. It was only in the truck that she allowed her composure to falter. "It isn't her, and she was our best lead."

He turned the truck toward the police station

and her work. "There will be other leads. We'll just have to find them."

"We?" When he looked at her, her eyes were very blue, very vulnerable.

"Yes. *We.* I wouldn't leave you to face this on your own. We're going to find who did this to you." He didn't add the words *before it's too late,* but they hung in the air anyway.

NINE

Later that afternoon, as she was working in her office, Gracie couldn't stop thinking about Shay Smith. She'd always thought her job had been about getting resolution for the victims. She hadn't really thought that maybe, by taking away their excuses, she was doing the perpetrators a favor.

The phone rang on the desk in front of her, startling her out of her thoughts. "Gracie VanDoren."

"Gracie. It's Maria. I got the results of the DNA testing we were doing on those samples from your house."

"And?"

"Well, the results are pretty interesting. I stepped out for lunch, but I'm on my way back to the lab. Want to meet me there?"

"Sure." Gracie grabbed her ID and headed

for the elevator. She met Maria on the ground floor.

Maria had on her cargo pants, boots and a long-sleeved cotton T-shirt. She kept the lab at a cool sixty-five degrees—better for evidence—so even in the summer, she tended to wear long sleeves under her lab coat.

Maria stepped forward to slide her ID card through the slot at the lab door. The doors hissed open. "Ah, love that sound. The entrance to my universe, where I am the queen."

Gracie smiled. "Does your husband know you want to be the queen?"

"Yes. He even gave me a tiara, which I am allowed to wear one day a week." Maria slid into a desk chair and shot a grin over her shoulder as her fingers flew on the keys. "Okay, here we go. Here's the DNA sample that belongs to you that we had on file."

She clicked the mouse and the screen changed to a new set of lines. "Here's a gray hair that came from a hairbrush in the master bathroom. Looking at the DNA results compared to yours, probability shows it belonged to your father."

A hard swallow got rid of the lump in Gracie's throat. So many traces of her dad were still in that house. Right down to DNA. "Is there anything else?"

"Yep. This is the interesting one." Maria moved the mouse again and another result appeared, this time with the hair in a split-screen.

"Here's the blood sample we took from the tubing in the stove. We're waiting for the retest to confirm, but the results are pretty clear."

Gracie shook her head. "I don't understand."

"Oh—sorry. Markers indicate that the DNA sample is from a half-sibling. *Your* sibling."

The room began to gray around the edges. "That's not possible."

"Like I said, I'm retesting to be sure, but this kind of result is not likely to change." Maria clicked the computer screen and looked back. "Gracie, are you all right?"

She shook her head and gripped the lab table, trying to stay upright. "I'm an only child."

That statement stopped Maria mid-motion. "Oh Gracie, I'm sorry. I could've broken the news a little easier."

"No, it's fine. You didn't know. Is there no other explanation?"

"I'm sorry, no. Since we have your father's

DNA, too, we get a much clearer picture." Maria put the computer to sleep and turned to Gracie. "Listen, I'll triple-check it."

"You said that it wasn't going to change. I have a sibling. And that sibling broke into my house and, what, cut the hose on the gas stove? Really?" It didn't seem possible—not even in the realm of possibility. She shook her head. "I've got to go. Just keep me posted, okay?"

She could feel Maria's eyes boring into her back as she waited for the elevator. Her chest hurt with every breath. How? How could she have a sibling—one she'd never imagined existed, much less heard of?

The doors to the elevator opened and she stepped inside, pressing the button for her floor and leaning against the wall. Her legs felt rubbery, like all the structure had given way. Which made sense because her structure, her foundation, had just completely been undermined with one word. *Sibling.*

The doors opened again on the first floor. Gracie pushed through the people waiting to get on. Forget going to her office. She needed air.

How could she not know? Another person existed on the earth who had at least a portion

of her own DNA and she hadn't had a clue.
Her father had another child. A daughter.

Shaking fingers reached for her necklace,
the ring he'd given her. Telling her not to date,
to save herself, now that was priceless. In the
parking lot, she leaned against her car. Warm
sunshine poured through the trees. She could
feel it on her shoulders, but it didn't seem to
be getting through. A shadow fell over her.
She shivered.

"Gracie? What's going on?"

"Go away, Tyler. I'm fine."

"You don't look fine. You look pale. What
happened?" He leaned against the car beside
her and peered at her face.

"It's...not something I want to talk about
right now. Maybe later. I've got to get back to
work."

She took two steps toward the building and
then turned back.

Given his line of work, of course he had
questioned who he was. But what made her
situation different was that her father had
been the one feeding her the pack of lies. She
breathed an exasperated sigh and, shaking her
head, backed away.

He reached for her hand, not grabbing it
but just resting hers in his. "Come on, Gracie,

what's going on? You know you can tell me anything."

"I just found out that the hair they picked up at the house belongs to my sister."

"Oh." He looked down at their hands, and then as her words sank in he looked back at her face. *"Oh."*

"Right. Which doesn't make sense because I'm an only child. My mom died when I was thirteen. If I have a sister, that means my dad had an affair. And the evidence is really incontrovertible. I have a sister."

"So that news had to be a shock to you." Tyler's voice held a note of caution.

The anger she'd expected to feel wasn't there. Instead, she just felt sadness. A void. "You could say that. My dad always insisted that I should wait to find my best friend, my one true love, before getting married. I thought my parents were devoted to each other in spite of the fact that he traveled so much. I thought when he said those things that he was talking about my mom."

"Maybe he was. It's possible, right?"

She shrugged impatiently. "I guess."

Her hand was still in his. He walked toward a small bench under an oak tree and sat studying her with that intense way of his.

Gracie blew out a frustrated breath and

pushed to her feet. "I don't know. I just keep thinking about the twins and their dad the other day. He promised them that they'd be together. He was so desperate to be with them that he would do anything, absolutely anything, including holding your brother hostage, to make it happen."

Tyler picked up the ID she left sitting on the bench and followed her with it.

"And there's a part of me that wonders how many fathers would go to that extreme for their kids. Would mine?" She turned back to him. "Never mind. I'm obviously still emotional about the whole thing."

Tyler's expression was a mixture of concern and determination as he reached for her collar and clipped her ID to her shirt. "We're going to figure this out, Gracie. Look at it this way—this morning when we crossed Shay Smith off our list, we didn't have any leads. Now we know exactly where to start looking. Right?"

"Right." She sighed heavily. "I'm going to make a call to my father's accountant. If my father had another child that he knew about, his accountant would've known."

The next morning, the thick envelopes hit Gracie's desk with a thud, startling her out of a paperwork-induced coma. She glared at the young Police Explorer who, as part of his volunteer duties, delivered the mail.

"Sorry, Doc. Didn't mean to startle you." The teenager shot her a toothy grin.

She narrowed her eyes at him and he left. As he rolled his cart down the hall to scare some other unsuspecting mail recipient, she observed the packages. They had cleared the mailroom, so there wasn't anything too terribly threatening about them.

Gingerly, she turned the top one over and gave a huge sigh of relief when she realized the envelopes had been couriered over from her father's accounting firm.

Judging by the size of these packages, she was going to need help. She reached for the phone and then hesitated. Then reached again and dialed the extension for Maria Fuentes Storm.

Two hours later, she was sitting at the farm table in Maria's kitchen with the financial reports spread between the two of them and a headache growing behind her left eye. An ice-cold diet soda dripped sweat onto a napkin as she stared at another page of incomprehensible payouts. The inner workings of a person's psyche, body language, secrets and lies...all these she was comfortable discerning. Numbers, not so much.

Maria pushed a plate of whole-wheat banana bread across the table. "You look like you could use some sustenance."

"Did you make it?" Gracie looked at it with suspicion, but she broke off a piece of cake and laid it on the napkin by her soda.

"I could've made it, if I'd wanted to." Maria held Gracie's gaze for a long second and then laughed. "Okay, okay. I hate that you can always tell when I'm lying. Caden's nanny made it. You're safe."

"It seems a little strange thinking about you with a little boy. Do you like it?"

"Love it. He's the most awesome kid ever. And I haven't announced it at work yet, but we just found out we're expecting another one."

"Maria, that's terrific." Gracie reached across the table with her drink to clink Maria's glass.

"I know. Six months ago, I didn't know Ben Storm existed, other than to sneer at him on television." She looked around at a room clearly designed for a family. Gracie followed her gaze to a line of cars on the windowsill closest to the fireplace. "I'm telling you, God has an amazing sense of humor and an astounding capacity for blessing."

Gracie's lips trembled as she smiled, but she firmed them. She wasn't jealous of Maria, but she was old enough to have real longings for that dream of a husband and family, the toy car parking lot on the windowsill.

She loved her job, loved the people she worked with and her friends. But when she'd been younger and had pictured her life, she'd always pictured herself with a husband and little children. Maybe that was her dream and not God's plan for her. And maybe that was something she would have to come to grips with, but for now, she needed to focus on following the money trail to figure out what her father had been up to.

The door slammed open and a small boy hurtled through the space. A blurred impression of two sturdy little legs and red Converse tennis shoes were what she got until she saw him take a flying leap into Maria's arms.

"Hey, bud. How was play group?"

"I bounced the green ball fourteen times in a row."

"Awesome. What else?"

"Mrs. Mack tried to make me put all the square blocks into a round hole, but I told her they would only fit in the square hole. Can holes be square, Mom?"

"Good question, Caden. Hey, do you remember Doc? Will you say hello, please?"

With a small sort of scowl at being interrupted, Caden looked up and met her eyes for a fleeting second. "Hi."

As he buried his face in her shoulder, Maria gently extracted it. "Where's Julia, Caden?"

"Right here. I had to get the evidence out of the car." A young woman with short brown hair came in the front door. She lifted a smoothie cup from a local store. "But he did really well, so he deserved a special treat. And now we both need a really long rest. Right, Caden?"

"I don't think so."

Julia looked at her watch and pointed to a brightly colored chart on the fridge. "The time says one-oh-oh and that's rest time on your calendar. See?"

He slid off of Maria's knees and looked back at her, his bottom lip poking out. "I don't like that calendar."

"I know, bud." Maria's eyes were shining with amusement. "Go get a clean shirt on and I'll come read you a story."

Gracie laughed as Caden walked as slowly

as possible toward the door to the hall. "He's doing so well."

Maria nodded. "Autistic spectrum disorders are a mixed bag in any case, but he makes improvements every day. I'm sorry to leave you, but I try to spend as much time with him as possible on my days off."

"Of course you do. I'll be right here." As Maria sped toward the hall, Gracie picked up the next page in her stack and fought the disheartening feeling she got when she looked at all those numbers. Surely there was a clue in here somewhere, but these records went back twenty-five years. It was like trying to find a four-leaf clover in a field full of the stuff. All the numbers looked legitimate.

Wait. There was the record of a mortgage payment for a house in Sedona. Her father had done a lot of work in Arizona developing neighborhoods, but she hadn't realized that he'd bought a house there. The extent of what her father had owned over the years sometimes appalled her, mostly because she had no idea the scope of it all.

It could be that he bought the house simply because it was more prudent than staying in a hotel on his many business trips, but it could be the clue she'd been looking for.

She picked up the phone and called her father's attorney, the one who handled the will after her father died. The assistant put her through immediately, and when she heard the warmth in the voice of one of her father's oldest friends, she had to swallow back tears.

"Henry, I know this might seem like a weird question, but did Daddy leave any other bequests that I didn't know about?"

There was silence on the line. Then her father's attorney cleared his throat. "Why do you ask? Are you afraid there was some misappropriation of funds or property?"

"No, Henry, not at all. But there's a house in Sedona worth one point two million dollars listed among my father's assets. I can't find a record that it ever sold, but I don't remember that it was in the final settlement either."

The elderly attorney cleared his throat again. "I don't think that this matter falls under attorney-client privilege anymore. Your father never asked that I keep the bequests from you…he just asked that they be kept separate."

Blood rushed in her ears. Could it really be this simple?

"Let me find it, dear." She could hear keys

typing over the phone line. "Okay, here it is. The house was left to a Regina Graham. And there was a monetary gift, as well. Five hundred thousand dollars."

She let her breath out slowly. "Wow. Okay. That seems a little bizarre. Do you know any details? Why he would do that?"

"Honey, I can't tell you anything more, I'm sorry. I know he did the best he could to live up to his responsibilities."

That didn't help.

"Thanks, Henry. I promise it won't be as long before you hear from me again."

As she hung up the phone, she pulled her laptop open and typed the name into a search engine. Regina Graham. It seemed so strange to see a woman's name in connection to her father. To know nothing about this woman at all, not even that she existed.

Within a few seconds, there were a dozen pages of hits. Regina Graham was an artist, a few years younger than Gracie's father, and she still lived in Sedona. Gracie looked up the address for the county records website, and when she had the right search function she entered the address.

Yes, Regina Graham still owned the house on Canyon Creek Road. And Gracie needed to talk to her. She took a deep breath. It meant going to Arizona. Facing a part of her father's life that she preferred to never, ever explore.

Her chair teetered on its legs as she shoved away from the table. She had to get out of here, had to figure out the next step. To do that, she needed space.

She grabbed the sheets from the printout that she needed and her purse and started for the door, leaving the rest of the papers scattered on the table. Maria came to the hall door as she was reaching for the knob.

"Hey, sunshine, I'm done with the munchkin, and if you want to spend another hour with your eyes crossing, I'll make a pot of coffee."

"I've got to go. I'll get the papers from you later. Thanks—for everything."

Gracie wrenched the door toward her and barreled through it, gulping air as she hurried to her car.

TEN

Where was Gracie? Her car was in the driveway, but she wasn't answering the door. She wasn't answering her phone either. She wasn't at the main house because he'd looked there, too.

Tyler'd about decided to kick down the door to her pool house and risk the crazy alarm that Wonder-geek had installed when, through the window, he saw a pair of her shoes by the bedroom door. He thought to look in the soft gravel and sand near the edge of the sidewalk. There it was—the print of a running shoe.

Feeling reasonably sure that she'd gone running, he started down the driveway. Maria had said that Gracie'd been upset, but she hadn't been able to figure out what it was that had sent her running out the door.

As he got to the end of the long curving driveway, he saw her. She slowed to a stop and leaned over, catching her breath and timing her pulse with her fingers on her neck and her eyes on her watch.

Tyler opened his mouth to call her name as he walked toward her. And barely reacted in time to dodge her fist before it connected with his chin. "Easy, Gracie, it's me."

"Tyler, what are you doing here?"

"Maria called me. She was worried about you."

"She shouldn't be."

"Did you find something?" he asked.

Gracie dropped onto a concrete bench set into the woods. Who had that kind of stuff, just sitting around in the woods? People who had enough money to have the woods around their house landscaped, that's who.

She grabbed a flyaway curl poking her forehead and smoothed it back into her ponytail. "I did. I'm just not sure what to do about it. My dad bought a house in Sedona for a woman who's still listed as the owner."

"Do you think she knows what this is all about?"

Gracie stared up into the canopy of tiny green spring leaves. "Maybe. She's the right age to have a daughter with my dad."

Tyler watched her. There was something

going on inside that mind of hers, something eating at her. He didn't say anything, just waited for her to want to share it. Or not.

"Do you know why I live in the pool house, really?"

"I don't have a clue. I figured that it was because the main house is so big and empty without your dad."

"That's part of it." She stared down the road for a long minute before continuing. "My dad was gone so much when I was young and my mom hated that big house. I didn't understand it then. I had the most beautiful room and everything I wanted…" Her voice trailed off.

"But?"

"But now I guess I understand. I love that house, but it isn't mine."

"Your dad left it to you."

"I know. And I need to decide what to do with it, but for now, I'm living in the pool house because it fits who I am now."

"And we're talking about this because…"

"For several reasons, but for one, I'm thinking about asking my father's partner if we can use the plane to get to Arizona." She made a rueful face.

"You have a plane?"

"My father's company owns a plane. It's not mine."

"I see."

"Do you?"

"Of course I do, Gracie. You don't want to depend on your father's money any more than I wanted to depend on my father's reputation as a cop. I had to do it my own way. Do you think I wouldn't respect you for doing things yours? Come on." He stood and held out a hand to her.

"Where are we going?" She took his hand and he pulled her to her feet.

"I'm making you dinner. You're tired and cranky and you need some sustenance. Then you can make the call to your father's partner or pilot or whoever it is you have to contact."

"Thanks."

"And I'm going with you. There's no telling what you'll find in Arizona."

"That's very reassuring."

"I'm here to help." He nudged her with his shoulder. "Come on, I'll teach you how to make my favorite pasta sauce. Garlic is good for whatever ails you."

"You know, if you keep cooking for me, you're going to spoil me." She smiled then, her eyes brightening.

Oh, yeah. He was definitely going to try.

* * *

It had been years since Gracie had been on a plane with her father. She was pretty sure this one had been upgraded since then. She didn't remember the plane looking like a high-class boardroom. She didn't remember gleaming mahogany and plush velvet and leather seating. And she definitely didn't remember the lake-sized bed through the double doors at the back of the airplane.

Her feet stalled out. She couldn't stop staring at it. Why had this seemed like a good idea? That's right, it hadn't. It was awkward and awful. Totally not her by any stretch of the imagination.

Tyler crossed in front of her and slid the doors closed with an audible snap. "You have enough to worry about. Sit down. We'll be in the air in a few minutes."

She sat. As far away from the bedroom as possible in one of the bucket seats.

Tyler sat next to her and reached around her to buckle her seat belt as the pilot started to taxi down the runway. "Distracted much?"

"I feel like I've been dropped into an alternate universe. One where my father kept secrets, I have siblings I don't know about and I'm using my father's money for a personal quest." Gracie ran her finger down the stitching of the leather seat. "And then to top it all off, I'm sitting here with you. It's really all too much."

He quirked an eyebrow at the last but didn't say anything for a few seconds. "It'll still be weird after this trip, but at least you'll have answers. As far as the fact that you're sitting here, next to me, you may as well get used to that. I'm not going anywhere."

"Why do you think that?"

"I don't know, Gracie." The exasperation in his tone amused her, but he hesitated. She could see it in his eyes. Despite everything, she was still a psychologist after all.

"'I don't know' is a cop-out answer, Tyler. What's the real one?" The engines of the plane roared and the force of the takeoff pushed her against the seat.

He rubbed the nonexistent stubble on his jaw. "I worked with a lot of different people in the DEA, and a lot of them I liked. But there are only a handful that I would call friends. I think you and I are getting close to being real friends, and I don't want to mess it up."

She didn't smile. Surprisingly, there was a tender place there, and she hadn't realized it. The guys at the precinct had eventually gotten used to letting her keep her personal life personal, and her relationship with them was more along the lines of little sister-big brother. Not even really friends, though if she'd been asked, even a couple of days ago, she would've said she had tons of friends.

Most men she met were so freaked out by the idea of her not dating that they didn't try. Tyler had taken her "no" and figured out a way around it. Figured out a way to build a friendship. "Why did you choose me? I mean, I know you were required to come for the appointment, but what made you pursue the relationship?"

"Hmm. I think it was the smiley face on the door of your office. It ticked me off."

A laugh snorted out, despite her effort to keep it in. "So you wanted to be friends?"

"No." He dipped his head, not meeting her eyes. "You put a smiley face on the whiteboard outside your office."

She was at a loss. "You liked my smiley?"

"I wanted to know what you have inside that, despite everything you do, would give you that kind of joy." He shrugged. "Nobody said it had to make sense."

He'd been playing her the first day they met,

feeding her the party line. She'd seen it in his face.

But he wasn't playing her now. She didn't say anything. Anything she thought of just sounded cheesy and trite. Without giving herself time to think about it, she reached for his hand and laced her fingers through his.

Tyler squeezed her hand and rubbed her finger with his thumb. She took a deep breath, the contact giving her comfort, the tightness in her chest easing. "Turns out I needed a friend, too."

The captain stepped through the cockpit door. "I'm Rob Coburn, your pilot. Miss Van-Doren, it's a real pleasure to have you aboard today."

"Thank you, Rob. About what time will we be in Sedona?"

"Flying time is around four hours from here. We'll have you on the ground safe and sound before you know it."

Safe and sound?

She hadn't had many moments that she'd felt completely safe since her father's house had been broken in to. She'd had moments when she forgot about it—briefly—but security seemed like a thing of the past.

And that was just what she was going to find

out about from Ms. Regina Graham. The past. No matter how painful or awkward it would be to ask the questions, she needed answers.

The adobe house in the middle of the desert seemed about as foreign as anything Gracie had ever seen. It was huge and multilayered. And compared to the rich blues and greens of the beach landscape, the colors of the house in its desert surroundings seemed stark.

"Ready?" Tyler's hand was poised to knock on the giant carved door.

"I'm not sure, but we didn't come all this way to stand on the porch." She blew out a breath. "Go ahead."

Tyler knocked and they stood there for a long couple of minutes. No one came to the door.

"Surely we didn't fly across the country for no one to be home. Maybe we should've called first."

"That would've involved planning." Tyler's voice was dry.

"Funny, but now we're going to need a plan." As she spoke, the door swung open. A woman, somewhere around forty, maybe fifty, stood in the opening. She had long black hair with one streak of white in the front.

She looked at Tyler first, but when her gaze

landed on Gracie, she sucked in a quick involuntary breath.

"Ms. Graham, I'm Gracie VanDoren."

"I've seen your picture. You look like your father."

"I'd like to talk to you for a few minutes, if you have the time." Gracie's fingernails dug little half-moons into her palm.

"I'm not sure dredging up the past is a good idea." The woman started to close the door.

Gracie put a hand on the door. "Please. You have a daughter."

Regina Graham stopped mid-motion. Then the door swung open again. She sighed. "Come on in."

The house was incredibly beautiful, the décor obviously influenced by the area, with rich, earthy colors complementing the adobe house. The aroma of incense filled the air. But what stunned Gracie was the view from the back windows. A wide expanse of crystal-blue sky with the majestic Red Rocks in the distance.

"Have a seat. Is iced tea okay?" Regina's hands were paint stained and shook, Gracie noted, as she fixed their refreshments. She wasn't as unaffected by Gracie's presence as she appeared to be.

"I appreciate you taking time out of your day for this, Ms. Graham."

The woman her father had...loved...sat down at the table across from her. "You met my daughter?"

Tyler's eyes, so dark and expressive, flicked up to meet Gracie's. *Careful,* they warned.

"I didn't know about the two of you, Ms. Graham. I found you by going through some of my father's papers. But I do believe your daughter is in my hometown. Maybe for the same reason that I'm here. Looking for some answers."

She believed that Regina's daughter was looking for more than that. Closure. Maybe even revenge. But for now, she needed to keep that speculation to herself.

Regina took a long sip from her glass of tea. "I met your father nearly thirty years ago. Honestly, I don't remember if I didn't know he was married or if I didn't care." A faraway look crossed her face. "He was handsome and passionate. The total opposite of my hippie self. I worked at a diner near the hotel where he stayed when he was here working on the developments in those days."

It was harder to hear than Gracie had imagined it would be. "You had an affair?"

"For a year, every time your father was here, we were together. I loved him, Gracie, that much you should know. And he loved me." Her voice dropped a notch. "Then without any warning, he broke things off. He sent his partner out here to work and he stayed in Florida. That was the year Hurricane Earline hit the coast there."

"The year I was born."

Regina nodded. "I didn't know that then. What he didn't know was that after he left, I found out I was pregnant. And I definitely wasn't telling him after he left me cold."

"I'm so sorry." She certainly could understand what Regina must've felt, alone and pregnant, with the man she'd trusted having left her.

Tyler reached for Gracie's hand under the table, gripping it in his. He wasn't letting go. Gracie's throat closed. She hadn't known what it would be like to be here, and knowing Tyler had her back made all the difference.

"Daphne didn't know who her father was until she was a teenager. One day, he appeared at the door, much like you just did. He'd discovered that he had a daughter and he wanted to make amends. He bought us this house and took her on trips. She adored him."

Gracie picked up on a slight hesitation in Regina's voice. "Until?"

"It wasn't until he died that Daphne found out that your father had another daughter, a daughter the same age as she is, a daughter who got to have him her whole life. She was already grieving for him, and then she found out there was another person who had the life she thought should've been hers." Regina ran her finger down the condensation on the outside of her glass. "She's always been dramatic, but this sent her over the edge. She left a month ago without any word."

Gracie didn't know what to say, which wasn't at all normal for her. She was the one with the answers, the one with the correct question in every situation. But faced with this mother's pain as she was dealing with her own insecurity, well, it was just too much to take in at once.

Tyler carefully placed his glass on the coaster Regina had given him. "Do you have any idea what she might want to achieve by coming to Sea Breeze?"

"I honestly don't know. There's a sweet side to her, you should know that. But she's bottled up anger for so many years, first from not having the father she thought she should have and then losing him." Regina's eyes were full, but the tears didn't fall. "I'm not sure she can get past it, not without help, and right now, she doesn't know how to ask for it—or want to."

Gracie stood. From a theoretical standpoint, she could understand Daphne's feelings, but this wasn't a theoretical situation, not for her.

She walked to a baby-grand piano in front of a large picture window. Picture frames of all sizes filled the surface. Most were of Regina's daughter from the time she was a chubby-faced toddler to a teenager with braces and frizzy brown curls. A few included Gracie's father. Those were the ones she wanted to see.

What kind of man had a secret family?

A photograph caught her eye. It looked like the photo she had of herself with her father in Yellowstone. For good reason. It was taken at exactly the same place at the same angle, except it wasn't her in the picture—it was her father and his other daughter.

Regina's voice at her shoulder startled her. "He took her on that trip for her fourteenth birthday. It was her favorite memory of the two of them."

She nodded, her throat too tight for words.

He'd taken her for her fourteenth birthday, too. Her father had not been the man she thought she knew.

Almost as if Regina had read her mind, she said, "He was a good man, Gracie. Maybe he was conflicted about the consequences of the choices that he made, but he tried to do his best for you and your mother. And once he knew about Daphne, he tried to do his best for her, too."

Gracie set the picture back in its place on the piano and picked up her purse, ready to leave. "Thank you for seeing us, Regina. I know this couldn't have been easy for you."

"I know you have questions, just like my daughter does." She handed them a slip of paper with Daphne's phone number and make and model of car. "I hope you find her. When you do, would you mind contacting me to let me know?"

"Of course." As the door closed behind them, Gracie couldn't help but look back at the house her father had built. He'd built this problem, too. And he wasn't here to fix it.

Tyler placed his hand at her back as they walked down the sidewalk to the rental car. It was warm and reassuring. She wanted to turn into him and let him hold her, let him make promises that he had no way of keeping just to make her feel better.

"Was it better hearing about in person?"

"I think it made it more real, to see a house that my father lived in with another family, to meet his…whatever she was. Everywhere I looked, I could imagine him. It was very strange."

"What's the next step?"

"Besides going home? I need to find Daphne and talk to her face-to-face. This has to end."

As they pulled into the airport and parked the car, Tyler reached for her hand. She looked down at their fingers. His strong, calloused fingers linked with her smaller, smoother ones. Other than Tyler, she'd never held hands with a man besides her father. She cherished the sensation of their palms together. This connection felt right somehow.

However, she needed to take this very slowly. What she was feeling could be for a number of reasons, not the least of which was gratitude for him sticking by her.

Take the fact that he didn't know what he wanted to do with the rest of his life. Take the fact that she barely knew who she was anymore. And take the fact that both of their emotions were heightened because there was someone trying to, at worst, kill her, and, at best, scare her silly.

But oh, she did feel better when he was holding her hand. She looked out over the runway. "We'll be home in a few hours. Tomorrow morning I have court, but after that I'll try to put some time in searching rental properties for any trace of Daphne. She's been in Sea Breeze a couple of weeks. Someone has to have seen her."

Heat radiated from the tarmac as they walked toward the airplane. And heat radiated up her arm from his hand through hers.

"Sounds good. We can start after lunch at Finn's tomorrow?"

She smiled, his solidarity unexpectedly soothing the rawness inside of her after the talk with Regina. "Are you sure you want to do that? I know you have a job starting soon."

"Tired of me already?" His voice held just a hint of insecurity and she turned to him, searching his face for a clue to the reason.

"I'm sure I could have handled this on my own if I had to." She touched his arm. "But I'm really glad I don't have to."

Walking into the plane, she met their pilot

ducking out of the cockpit. "Miss VanDoren, we've found a small problem with the starter. Unfortunately, we'll have to stay here until the part can be located and replaced. I've taken the liberty of making reservations for both of you at the Sedona Rouge. I'm so sorry for the inconvenience. We'll leave at first light and have you back at home by noon." The pilot handed Tyler a packet of information about the Sedona Rouge. "There's a car waiting for you at the gate."

Tyler looked at Gracie. She hadn't moved. He shrugged. "I guess we'll be staying the night. The resort probably has shops where you can find the necessities."

She grabbed her computer bag from beside the chair where she'd been sitting on the flight to Sedona and checked the strap on her shoulder, he assumed to make sure she still had her purse. "Okay, let's go. I need to make some calls and reschedule my court date. Maybe they can push it back to after lunch tomorrow. What a mess."

Less than an hour later, he'd left her on the public terrace of the resort with her laptop, a cup of herbal tea and an incredible view, while he went to find a clean shirt for the next day. He browsed through a few shops but ended up with a golf shirt from the resort for himself and a bag of stuff the lady at the shop put together for Gracie.

She'd asked what size Gracie wore. He had no idea. She was small. She liked skirts. The salesperson had laughed at him, but in the end it hadn't been that painful. The woman held up two skirts. Tyler pointed to the one he thought Gracie would like.

Talk about outside his comfort zone. But this journey he was on was about discovery. Or so he kept telling himself.

He walked back to the terrace with the bag in his hand and reservations at REDS for dinner. "Hey there, I've had a productive hour. How about you? Did you get your schedule worked out?"

When she looked up, he could see from her expression that everything had not worked out. It was a mixture of anger and fear.

He pulled out the chair across from hers at the small table. A server immediately stepped up to the table. Tyler waved him away. "What happened?"

She stared at the distant mountains, glowing in the twilight. "Someone hacked into my Facebook account. Posted as me."

A cold feeling settled in his stomach that

had nothing to do with the chill in the air. He turned the computer screen. "Let me see."

Her status read, *Gracie Clark is putting her friends and loved ones in danger. And NO ONE can protect them.*

"You need to stay away from me." Her bottom lip trembled and she clamped down on it with her teeth.

"Do you really think that I would?"

Her eyes were huge in her face. "You should."

"There's no amount of threats that could make me leave you alone." He closed the computer. "Come on, let's go get dinner. I made reservations."

Despite herself, she gave a sort of half laugh and stood as he held out his hand. "Food makes everything better?"

"Something like that. Especially if the food is really good." But as he tucked her laptop under his arm, he had a cold feeling that there was no amount of food that could make this go away. By making threats, her sister was taking this to the next level.

And from experience, Tyler didn't think there were going to be any easy answers.

ELEVEN

The flight home was quiet. Too quiet. There were dark circles under Gracie's eyes that hadn't been there yesterday, and her skin had a pale fragility that was very unlike the self-assured woman he'd met his first day at the precinct.

It was mid-afternoon by the time they reached Pensacola. As the pilot taxied the plane, Tyler looked out the window. He saw Cruse Conyers waiting for them on the tarmac, leaning on his car. That couldn't be good.

Cruse walked to meet them as they stepped off the stairs. "Welcome back to Florida. Eventful trip?"

"Plane trouble. Cruse, what's going on?" Gracie lifted the strap of her computer bag over her shoulder and walked toward the terminal.

Cruse swung into step beside her, keeping easy pace. "Did you visit Shay Smith recently?"

Gracie stopped. She turned and looked at Tyler. He didn't move but flicked his eyes to Cruse.

She put one hand on her hip. "Obviously, you know that I did. What's this about? Is her lawyer crying about it? She let me in voluntarily, Cruse."

"She was murdered sometime early this morning. Her boyfriend found her when he came to have breakfast with her around nine o'clock."

The news stopped them in their tracks. Tyler narrowed his eyes as Gracie gasped. "Oh, no. Cruse! She was really doing well."

"You have something to add, Clark?" Cruse looked at Tyler.

"I'm just thinking, sad as it is, this news could've waited. Why are you here?"

Cruse shifted his weight, looked at Gracie. "The perp used your letter opener. The only prints CSI found were yours."

"We were in Sedona until this morning. You can check the hotel records." Tyler said it before Gracie could. She didn't need to have to defend herself. But if they hadn't had plane trouble, she would've been a suspect. Maybe not a real suspect, but enough of a suspect to muddy the waters.

She turned and walked toward the terminal again. "She got into my office. Which means that she got into the police department, either dressed as me or as herself, and went into my office and stole the letter opener."

"She. We're talking about your half-sister?" Cruse pulled a notebook out of his pocket. "Does she have a name?"

Gracie paused. "Daphne VanDoren. But I don't know if that's the name she's using. She might be using her mother's name. Graham."

"Thanks. We'll see what we can find out. Keep in touch." Cruse walked back to his car, his cell phone already at his ear.

Tyler drove her home. She didn't say a single word on the thirty-minute drive and went straight to the pool house when they got back to the estate, barely pausing to say, "See you later." But he could see on the handheld monitor that Wonder-geek had given him that she was inside and her security system had been armed.

Minutes later, as he walked the perimeter of the house, making sure everything was still pinned down after their day away, he heard the rhythmic pounding of the treadmill in her spare room. He was beginning to figure her out. She ran when she needed to think. And she had definitely needed to think after the past couple of days. She'd been blindsided by the information that her father had a child—a life—she'd never known about. The fact that the same child had most likely killed Shay Smith and was probably trying to kill her, too, was a little much to assimilate.

Several hours later he stood at the window of the estate house kitchen, beginning the prep work for casseroles for the fire station, and he was still thinking about her. His hands were a blur on the cutting board as he chopped carrots with his chef's knife. The security monitor on the counter beeped, and in his peripheral vision he caught the quick gleam of a door being opened and closed at Gracie's house.

A dark figure darted down the path toward the bay.

Tyler dropped the knife on the counter and opened the kitchen drawer. He'd made a practice of keeping his handgun nearby when he was in the house. He sincerely hoped he wouldn't need it, but as things escalated around here, he'd decided that being prepared was better than being sorry.

Outside, the moon made a swath of light across the dark water of the bay and slightly illuminated the pier. He eased down the path until he could see her at the end, her feet dangling, bright curls shining in the moonlight.

Tyler stepped onto the wooden slats. His intention had been to join her, but maybe she just needed some time. No one could get to her without coming through him first.

"Come on out." The words drifted back, carried on the soft breeze across the water.

He looked down the sandy beach in either direction and didn't see any movement. It looked clear. Still a little uneasy, he tucked his gun into the small of his back and dropped his shirt over it. Handy, but not obvious.

At the end of the pier, he realized that Gracie was wearing running shorts and an old SBPD T-shirt. "Aren't you cold?"

"Not yet." She sighed. "Today was strange."

"Weird," he agreed, wondering where she was going with this.

"The worst part of all of this is that I feel lost. I thought I had everything figured out. That God had a plan for me and I was following it." Gracie kicked her dangling feet, not close enough to touch the water. "I keep praying that God will show me what I'm supposed to do with all this information, but I'm not getting any answers. It's like I'm out here all alone."

"Wilderness."

"What?"

"My mom calls those wilderness times. I think she gets it from the Bible, like when Jesus went into the wilderness and was tested, but there are lots of other people in the Bible who dealt with the same thing—dealing with something awful and feeling like God was nowhere to be found."

Her eyes glimmered with tears in the vague light of the moon, and he could barely see her chin tremble as she fought for control. "You mean, there might be a reason for all this?"

"You are so asking the wrong person, but...I think not being able to feel God's presence might be the point. We have to have faith that He's there, no matter what's going on."

Gracie sniffed. "You're really smart."

He laughed, and it sounded loud as it bounced across the water of the bay. "No, I'm not. Apparently God has needed to get my attention more than once. I'm familiar with wilderness times."

She turned toward him. Her curls were tossed in the wind, her eyelashes dark with tears, but there was something there, something so special about her. The soft slap of the water picked up speed as a fishing boat trolled by, echoing the increase in his heart rate as she looked at him.

Tyler slid a hand into her hair, curving it around her neck. She turned her cheek into his hand and closed her eyes.

His chest constricted. "You can't—" He had to stop and clear his throat. "You can't imagine how badly I want to kiss you right now."

Her lips parted as she opened her eyes. "I think I can. Imagine, I mean."

He leaned forward, drew in a breath of sweet coconut shampoo. She was so innocent. No way was he going to take advantage of that.

Drawing a ragged breath, Tyler reined in his scattered thoughts—and yeah, if he was honest, his raging hormones, too. He was a man and had the feelings that a man had toward a woman he was attracted to. He was still strong enough to walk away.

Maybe.

He took her hand. "Come on, let's get out of the moonlight before we do something crazy."

"Maybe I want to do something crazy." Her

voice was soft as she played with the fingers of the hand that she held.

Heat shot through him and again he reined it in. With effort. "Maybe. And maybe not. It's the 'maybe not' that's the kicker. When I kiss you for the first time, I want it to be with no regrets, nothing fueling it except that it's you and me."

"There's going to be a first time?"

He smiled and got to his feet, pulling her to hers. "Come on, let's get inside. You're starting to get chilled."

Gracie walked beside him down the pier and shivered. He put his arm around her.

"You're a nice guy, Tyler Clark."

"Yeah? Well, don't tell anybody."

When they reached the pool house, he leaned against the door frame as she unlocked the door. He made a quick tour of the house, but all was quiet. "I'll see you tomorrow afternoon. Call me if you need anything."

"I will." She gazed up at him. "Tyler, there's a lot of things to thank you for, but mostly for being a friend when I needed one today."

"Anytime." He waited for her to close and lock the door and arm the security system before starting back to the main house.

Tyler released the breath he'd been holding.

It had been close out there on the pier. He wanted to kiss her more than anything he could think of.

But he already knew something that sent cold fear through his veins. She was too important to him to risk. He wanted more—far more—than just a few kisses under the moonlight.

He wanted it all.

Gracie swung her car toward the precinct after her rescheduled court appearance. She had a few phone calls to make before she could meet Tyler.

The plan for the afternoon—finding her sister—made nervous elephants jump in her stomach. Forget butterflies. This was way bigger than that.

Her cell phone rang. She punched the button to answer it with her hands-free system. "Gracie VanDoren."

"Gracie, it's Tyler." His voice came through deep and rumbly, just like it was in person.

Her cheeks warmed, thinking about their almost-kiss last night. "What's up?"

"I have some news. With the information that Daphne's mom gave us about the type car she drives with the Arizona tag, I was able to come up with a possible location. Want to check it out?"

"Yes, where?"

Amusement laced his voice. "I see you're undecided about this."

"I want my cat."

Silence. "Gracie...we may not find Charlemagne. You should be prepared, in case he's not there."

"Tyler, where am I going?"

He named a group of apartments in a not-so-nice part of town. They rented by the month to seasonal workers, usually.

When she whipped into the parking lot, she found Tyler leaning on the bumper of his truck. Another tall, dark-haired man stood just apart from him, with his feet braced apart and arms crossed, almost as if he were on a boat.

Tyler stood when she walked up, but he took a half-step back.

"What?"

"You look...different. What's with the hair? And the suit?"

She looked down at the chocolate-brown suit and silky blouse she wore, along with the four-inch heels. She'd smoothed the curls out of her hair and wore it in a low chignon. "I have a PhD in psychology, Tyler. I know how to use my appearance to increase my credibility with judges and jurors."

A smooth lock of blond hair fell across her eye and she pushed it back impatiently, before holding a hand out to the other man standing nearby. "Hi, I'm Gracie."

"Gracie, my brother Ethan. He's law enforcement, here for backup." Tyler made the belated introduction as Gracie held Ethan's hand. And as he did, Gracie remembered. Ethan was the brother who lost his family in some kind of explosion.

So the lines on his face weren't simply from the sun, they were from grief.

"This is not exactly my jurisdiction, Ty." Ethan didn't smile.

"Well, there might be a cat involved. You're Florida Fish and Wildlife Commission."

Even Gracie knew that was stretching it. She also knew that Tyler's family had been extremely worried about Ethan. If she had to guess, she would say that Tyler dragged Ethan out under false pretenses in order to involve him in something, anything, other than work.

"I know you're joking." Ethan's voice was humorless.

Tyler's grin was a quick flash of white. "Come on, Ethan. Old times' sake."

"Old times' sake would mean that we would get caught, you would come out smelling like a rose and I would get grounded." But he started walking with them. "Do you have a plan?"

Gracie tipped her face up to look at Tyler. "A plan would be good, Tyler."

"How about we knock on the door?"

Gracie caught Ethan's eye behind Tyler's back. She thought she saw just a hint of amusement there. "That's the plan?"

"Well, we can't break in. Gracie works for the police department and, as we've already established, you are law enforcement."

The elephants were back in Gracie's stomach. "What are we going to do if she answers the door? Say, 'Hi, I'm your sister. Where's my cat?'"

Tyler pulled a navy-blue shirt from the backseat of his truck and slid it on, reaching back for a clipboard. "Her car's in the parking lot, but she still might not be here. Let's look around, talk to the neighbors and see what we can find out."

"Do I get a fake uniform?" She put her hands on her hips and didn't move.

He stopped and looked back at her, a slow

grin spreading across his face. "No. I don't think you'll need one. You've got plenty to work with."

Ethan released a long-suffering sigh. "You really don't need me here."

"Yes, we do. We need you to keep Tyler from getting arrested." Gracie walked toward the apartment, her high heels tapping on the asphalt. "But if my cat's in there, he's coming home with me."

Tyler knocked on the door of the ground floor apartment where Daphne VanDoren lived.

Gracie tiptoed through a weedy flower bed to peek in the window as Ethan walked to the neighbor's apartment and knocked. As she looked in the window, her stomach twisted in revulsion.

The walls had been sloppily painted in the same lime and turquoise as Gracie's home. The furniture was draped with white sheets to make it look like her own white furniture. Even down to the blue-and-green pillows on the sofa, the room was an off-kilter replica of hers.

"Tyler. C'mere."

Her eye traveled the length of the couch. She saw a loafer-clad leg sticking out from behind.

Oh, man, that didn't look good. "Tyler, hurry. You need to get a look at this."

He came around the corner and raised a hand to his eyes so he could see through the window without glare.

"Behind the sofa."

Tyler didn't say anything, but planes of his face settled into deep unhappy grooves.

"Well?"

He pulled his cell phone out of his pocket and began dialing. "I think now we might have reason to enter. Ethan?"

Ethan came around the corner of the apartment and took a quick look through the window. His eyes, already dark and serious, went even harder. He pulled out his service weapon and stepped back around the corner by the entrance to the apartment.

Tyler spoke quietly into the phone and then hung up. He slid it into his pocket and from the small of his back pulled his gun.

Adrenaline surged through Gracie as she followed him around the corner. He stepped to the opposite side of the door from Ethan and nodded. Gracie waited behind them, pressed against the wall.

Ethan knocked firmly on the door. "Miss VanDoren, this is the police. Does someone need help in there? Miss VanDoren, can you open the door, please?"

There was no sound in return.

He shrugged at Tyler. "Kick it in?"

Tyler sent him a look and tested the knob on the door. It twisted under his hand. He pushed the door open and stepped through the entrance.

Gracie's heart beat like mad inside her chest. The tension seemed unbearable. She saw Tyler motion to Ethan to check the body on the floor as he silently made his way toward the back of the apartment.

Ethan stooped to feel the neck of the guy on the floor. He glanced at her and shook his head.

From the back of the apartment, she heard, "We're clear."

Ethan, in his dark green uniform, waved her in. "Don't touch anything, okay?"

"I know. I've worked crime scenes before." She looked around at the run-down little apartment. "But this is just creepy."

"You don't know the half of it." Tyler walked out from the back room, her big orange cat in his arms.

"Charlemagne!"

"Careful. He's a little testy." Tyler had one long scratch down side of his face.

"Ooh, that has to sting."

"Shut up, Ethan." As he transferred the cat who was now purring and rubbing his face all over Gracie's, Tyler scowled down at the dead guy. "I told that guy he should leave town."

"Who is he?" Ethan snapped the holster around his weapon.

"The private investigator that Daphne hired to follow Gracie. Apparently she bashed him over the head."

"Is that the technical term for it?" Ethan's tone was dry, his face expressionless.

Gracie walked around the room trying to take things in as she listened with half an ear to the brothers' good-natured teasing, well used to cops bantering at crime scenes.

She snuggled her cat close, his soft weight a welcomed burden. She'd been afraid she would never see him again.

Tyler wrapped a long arm around his brother's neck. "Thanks for coming. You don't have to stay. I'll see you Saturday, right?"

"Right, Matt's wedding."

Grief flickered in Ethan's eyes, and Gracie's heart went out to him. Tyler held

Ethan's arm. "You are going to be at Matt's wedding, right?"

"Of course." Ethan pulled away and walked toward the door. "Mom would never forgive me if I missed it."

Gracie stopped Ethan on his way to the door. "Thanks for coming. We couldn't have done this without you."

He gave her a look like, *Yeah, whatever* and then leaned in. "I feel compelled to warn you. Tyler always has a way of getting what he wants. It appears he wants you."

"If you say so." Gracie hugged her cat closer.

The corner of Ethan's mouth tipped up, just for a second. "See you around. I'll hang around outside, give the detective my statement."

As sirens sounded in the distance, Tyler called from what she assumed was the bedroom. "You should come get a look at this."

She walked down the hall, feeling goose bumps prickle across her skin. She just wanted to escape this creepy off-version of her place. "What is it?"

"See for yourself." He stepped out of her line of sight and Gracie gasped, nearly dropping Charlemagne as she loosened her grip in shock.

The entire wall was plastered with pictures of her, dating back at least several weeks, because there were pictures of her running in long pants, and it had been that long since they'd had a cold snap. She shuddered at the thought that someone had been following her, snapping pictures, and she'd had no idea.

There were up-close shots of her clothes, her purses and shoes, her ID card. Her face, as she talked on her cell phone.

"I feel sick, Tyler. I think I might be sick." Her sister was doing everything possible to steal her life. Her hair, her decor, her stuff, her cat sitting in the window of her house. Her stomach rolled.

"Let's get out of here." He moved her quickly toward the door and down the hall.

Outside the front door of the house, they almost collided with Detective Joe Sheehan of the SBPD. While Gracie braced her hand against the brick wall and gulped air, Tyler reported to the cops what they had done and seen, that they hadn't touched anything except the door handle on the outside and the guy's neck to make sure he was dead. Well, and they had rescued Gracie's cat.

He stopped and stared at Daphne's car with its Arizona plates. "I guess it's possible that she might not have been involved, but my gut is telling me that she's behind this. I think she killed the private investigator and she's driving his van. That description should be on file from when you pulled him in."

"Got it. Will you ask Doc if she'll stay available tonight for me to ask some questions? This woman seems to have a serious thing for her."

"Will do." *A serious thing.* That seemed to be an understatement. A serious grudge, maybe. Tyler headed for his truck, his eyes on Gracie, whose shoulders were squared but who seemed to be having a hard time walking in a straight line. "Are you heading back to work?"

"I have to. I can't keep taking time off to deal with my personal issues, as much as I hate to leave him at home alone." She hefted her cat, who seemed determined to drool on her shoulder. "Stop that, Charlemagne."

Tyler eyed the beast. "I'll take him home for you."

"Are you sure you want to do that?" Guilt tinged her voice, her eyes lingering on the still-stinging scratch on his cheek.

"No, but he's had a hard few days. He

deserves to be home with his own litter box." Tyler held out his arms. Gracie shifted Charlemagne over and gave the feline a little scratch on the head.

It was pretty obvious that Charlemagne was not happy with his change of circumstance. He growled. The low kind of growl that made the hair on the back of Tyler's neck stand up. He gave the cat a wary look. "I'll see you back at the house. Around five-thirty?"

"You sure you're okay with this?"

"Yep, I'm good, but you might want to bring some antibiotic ointment home with you." He opened the door to his truck. The animal leaped in, turned around and gave Tyler a frightening look with his green cat eyes.

Gracie stopped halfway to her car, her face stricken. "I shouldn't leave you to deal with him."

Tyler closed the door so Charlemagne the King couldn't escape and walked to her, unwilling to let her leave worried and upset.

"I'm kidding, Gracie," he said gently. "Do your shrink thing and we'll meet back at the house. I promise, your cat will be treated like royalty."

She didn't move. "You're really sure."

"Yes. Now go." He watched her get into her

little car and drive away. She didn't deserve this. Especially considering that she was probably in more danger than they knew. Stalkers like this tended to go two ways. They either moved on to another object of their fixation, or they lashed out at the person at the center of their attention.

Daphne had already tried for Gracie once. She'd taken the bank accounts. She'd hacked into Gracie's Facebook page. They were assuming that she'd killed Shay Smith and now the P.I. It wasn't even a tiny step outside the realm of possibility that she'd go after Gracie. He pulled his cell phone out again. Cruse Conyers would make sure there was someone to meet her in the parking lot and walk her out when she left to go home.

He glanced across the street, feeling eyes on his back, but he didn't see anyone. He leaned against the truck and watched as Gracie turned the corner toward the police station.

Oh, God, please guard and protect Gracie. She's Your girl, and she needs You now. He felt a little silly, his skill at praying rusty at best, but somehow he didn't doubt that God was there.

An unearthly sound came from the cab of his truck. Now that was not a happy sound. But what could he do, except climb in with a very angry cat.

TWELVE

Late that night, Gracie placed the last dish in the dishwasher. Tyler had cooked a simple cassoulet. In her kitchen. She'd come home to find him asleep on the couch, her cat curled up on his chest, her house smelling like a home.

Of course he'd stayed for dinner. How could she not invite him? He'd pampered her cranky cat all afternoon, apparently winning Charlemagne over with a bowl full of tuna. That would do it.

The fact that he'd done it still floored her.

As she closed the dishwasher, she saw Tyler's truck pull out of the driveway. She walked to the French doors, drying her hands on a dish towel. Where would he be going at this time of night?

She dialed the phone. "Hey, Tyler, what's up?"

"Is everything okay?" Concern tinged his tone.

"I was just wondering what you're doing."

"Nothing much. Thinking about going to bed soon. You?" Thinking about going to bed, her foot. He was out driving around on who knows what kind of mission. She could hear the road noise over the phone. "Really, bed? I could've sworn I just saw your truck pull out."

Silence.

Then, "You won't be alone. I asked a patrol officer to come by and keep an eye on you."

"Okay, if that's the way you want it," she replied.

"Is everything locked up tight?"

It was really hard to hold on to her annoyance when he was being so concerned. "Yes, Tyler, everything is locked up tight. I'll see you tomorrow morning."

"Good night, Gracie."

She clicked the phone off, trying to fight off the disappointment. He was a good man. She'd seen that in his eyes the first time she met him. But she'd also seen the shadows there. Seen that he was carrying things with him that no one should carry. In the past week, she knew that he was discovering parts of himself that he hadn't known were there. He was committed to making a change in his life.

But she wondered how much his thinking patterns had been changed by life undercover. And how long it would take for him to realize that this life didn't require misdirection and equivocation.

She wasn't mad at him. He'd rescued her cat and had done everything he possibly could to help her. But he was lying.

And she wanted to know why.

Tyler walked out of the house the next morning and stopped cold. Gracie was sitting at the table on the back porch with a pot of coffee and two mugs, one already full of tea.

"Good morning. You look tired." Her golden curls shimmered as the rays from the early-morning sun shot through the trees. She didn't look tired at all.

She smiled up at him. "Want coffee? I didn't make breakfast, although I guess I could bring out some bran squares and milk."

He shook his head, let the smile come. She was always making him do that, even when he didn't feel like it. She'd obviously bought coffee for him. He had a sneaking feeling that she wasn't waiting for him on the back porch to have a nice chat about the weather, but still, she made him smile.

Pouring a cup of coffee, he sat in the iron chair beside her and stretched out his legs. He'd only gotten a couple of hours of sleep. Tired was an understatement.

"Where did you go last night?"

Sometimes he forgot her skill at asking the right question at the right time. He'd gotten a call about the PI's van from one of the cops he knew. "I went out for a drive. It wasn't a big deal."

She shook her head. "Truth, please."

He flicked his eyes up to meet hers. She didn't flinch, just gave him a measured stare. "Come on, Tyler. I observe interrogation as part of my job. You know I can spot a lie a mile away."

A muscle tightened in his jaw. He was supposed to be an expert at making people see what he wanted them to see. Was he losing his edge, or was she just that good? "I got a tip about the van we were looking for and thought I might be able to find where your sister is staying."

"Did you?" Irritation lingered just under the surface. He could see it around her eyes. It was so unlike her that he found himself fascinated by the signs.

"No. I backtracked different directions for hours from the spot where she was seen. I couldn't find her. I did manage to find a convenience store where she bought gas." He dug in his pocket and pulled out a grainy photograph and tossed it on the table.

Gracie picked it up, aversion crossing her face as she studied it. "She looks like me."

"She doesn't really. She's changed her appearance to try to look like you." He hadn't moved from his casually relaxed position in the chair. It bothered him just a little that she was questioning him, but he kept his position neutral.

"Do you know what irks me about you going last night?"

Irks? He was pretty intuitive, but honestly, women were beyond him. "Enlighten me."

"We have been working on this together, but when I called you last night, you lied to me about where you were going."

"It's not that—"

"I know you're good at it, but I didn't think you'd lie to me. I guess I was kidding myself."

"Gracie, I didn't want you to get your hopes

up." He didn't like being put in the position of defending himself.

"You've lied for so long in so many ways that I'm not sure you even recognize it. But until you figure out how to be honest with me all the time, I can't trust you."

A squad car pulled into the driveway, a uniformed officer behind the wheel. She waved.

"I'm not going to take any chances with my safety, don't worry. Officer Larson will drive me around today." She picked up her bag from beside her chair. "But if you have time this afternoon, I'd like to go back to the apartment where my sister was living and look at things more closely."

"I'll be at my mom and dad's helping out most of the day, but I can meet you there around four." With effort, he stayed in his seat instead of jumping to his feet to stop her from leaving.

"Thank you." She walked to the car, her signature skirt swishing around her knees, femininity a weapon she wielded with skill as she slid into the front seat beside the officer.

Exhaling sharply, he wondered if maybe she was right. Maybe he'd lied to hide his real feelings and what he really wanted. Maybe he hadn't told her because he was worried they were getting too close.

He hadn't realized he was doing it, but then again, she could be right about that, too. He'd been someone else for so long it was hard to separate the truth from the lies.

At his mom and dad's house, preparation was underway for the rehearsal dinner. Matt and Lara hadn't wanted anything fancy, opting instead for a cookout at Tyler's parents' house. Mom had decided against having her husband cook. As much as the sheriff would enjoy being the man in charge of the grill, hosting a party made it hard to cook.

So instead, she'd hired a catering group to come in and cook. They were making three different kinds of sliders and would have tables with cheese and fruit set up.

Tyler was in charge of the dessert. He'd made about a hundred and fifty mini red-velvet cupcakes, Matt's favorite. Those would be iced and topped with a small chocolate heart. He'd made the cupcakes in advance, and the hearts, so all he had to do was ice the cupcakes and put the toppers on.

His mom bustled into the kitchen. "I swear your father's going to be the death of me. He's decided to replant half the backyard. Today."

"Any other catastrophes that you need help averting?" He dumped softened butter into the mixer. Next would go the cream cheese and lots and lots of powdered sugar. The icing was simple but devastating when combined with the rich cake.

She poured herself a cup of coffee—her favorite french vanilla, he could smell it—and dropped into a chair. "Actually, I think everything's under control. I'm going to leave the caterers to their job. I'm going to let your father do whatever he wants, and I'm going to soak my aching feet."

With the first batch of icing complete, Tyler slapped some into a prepared pastry bag and began icing the first tray of cupcakes.

A few seconds later, his mother was at his elbow. "Ooh, pretty. I want to help."

"Mom, really, thanks, but no." When her face fell, he sighed. "If you want, you can stick the little chocolate hearts into the top of the icing."

She took one of the looped hearts that he'd piped the day before and stuck it into the icing. "Like this?"

"Perfect."

"I love this. I never would've expected the child who was always crawling through the underbrush to turn into such a genius in the kitchen." She placed some more of the hearts into the icing.

"Honestly, Mom, I wouldn't have expected it either. It just happened, and it fit."

"Well, honey, you look very manly with that pastry bag."

He laughed and shook his head, squeezing icing out of the tip of the bag with a firm hand and dabbing it on his mother's nose.

"I can still ground you, you know." She wiped her nose with the tip of her finger and tasted the icing. "Oh, sweetie, you really do know what you're doing. So tell me about Doc."

"There's nothing to tell."

She laughed and he could feel the heat climbing into his cheeks. Why was it that he could be cool as anything in the middle of a drug dealer's compound, but his mother asks him a simple question and he can't even meet her eyes? "What?"

"It's a sure sign that something is going on when you're so quick to say it's nothing." She took a swig of her coffee before she placed another row of little hearts on the cupcakes he'd already iced. "You said the same thing when you were fourteen and got caught kissing

Anna Louise Bernard behind the bleachers during the football game."

"Funny, Mom. To be honest, I don't know what's going on. I'm trying, really trying, to find my way back. I'm trying to make real relationships with people, like you and Matt and Marcus. Ethan. Gracie is a part of it, too." He piped icing onto another cupcake. "It's harder than I thought it would be."

"Things that matter usually are. Isn't she supportive?"

"Let's just say she's challenging me to be completely honest."

His mother's dark eyes were knowing. "And that's not always easy, not even between people who've been married as long as your father and I have."

He held her eyes a long time, somehow reassured by that fact. "I didn't expect to meet Gracie. Didn't expect to feel anything for anyone, not so soon. But she's important to me. What comes of it, well, I guess that's as much up to her as it is to me."

"You were always a quick study, Tyler. It used to make Matt furious how he had to work so hard for his grades and you could study for fifteen minutes and make all A's." She patted his back. "I think you'll figure out what you have to do."

Tyler kissed his mom on the forehead. "I will, thanks. Now go take your bath before it gets too late. I'll hold down the fort out here."

"You're bringing Gracie to the wedding tomorrow, aren't you?"

"I'll ask her if she wants to come."

"Good, you make sure she knows she's welcome." His mother's voice drifted back as she walked down the hall. "You make me proud, Tyler."

He sighed. He'd been a man for a while now, but his mother still had the power to bring him to his knees.

Gracie studied the apartment door where her sister had lived. Crime-scene tape crisscrossed the door and the crime scene lab had sealed the door, too. Officer Larson had planned to follow her over but had gotten a call. Tyler would be meeting her here. She would be fine.

A serious crime had been committed at this place. Not like breaking into her home. Not just stealing her cat—though in her book, that was bad enough.

This was worse even than the attempted

murder at her father's house. And as upsetting as Shay Smith's senseless death, a man had died here.

She couldn't yet think of the other woman as her sister, but there had to be something severely wrong with Daphne for her to be this obsessed with Gracie's life.

Gracie had been so overwhelmed with emotion yesterday that she hadn't really taken the time to look at the apartment. She hadn't studied it, not from a professional perspective, the way she was trained to do.

She heard a step behind her and whirled around. A woman, clutching what looked like a poodle mix, took a step back. "Something happened there. I knew that girl was bad news walking."

"Did you know her?" Gracie took two steps forward, and the woman, in her sweatpants and a big shirt, held her dog closer. Gracie held up her ID. "I'm Gracie VanDoren. I work with the police department."

"I'm Sherry. I live next door. That girl was coming and going at all hours of the night." The neighbor shrugged at Gracie's raised eyebrows. "The walls are thin. I could also tell you what kind of music she listened to."

"Did you hear anything the night before

last?" The medical examiner had discerned that the P.I. was killed the day before Gracie, Ethan and Tyler had found the apartment. It wouldn't have mattered if they'd found the location earlier in the day. It still would've been too late.

"No, I left Princess with my niece and took the red-eye bus trip to Biloxi to gamble with my Bunko group. I didn't get back until yesterday afternoon." The woman played with the dog's ear. "I told the other cops that, too."

"Have you thought of anything in the meantime?"

"No, but a package came for her today. The delivery man brought it to my door." The neighbor walked toward her apartment, the cuffs of her sweats dragging the ground. "I don't guess she's coming back for it. It's not like it was even regular U.S. mail either. A guy in a uniform brought it by, but there's no stamps. I thought it was weird."

"That does seem a little weird. May I?" Gracie hesitated at the threshold to the woman's apartment.

"Sure, come on in. Want some iced tea?" Sherry flipped through a short stack of envelopes on the counter.

"No, I'm good, thanks." Gracie looked

around the small apartment. The woman sure loved her animals. Little dog figurines filled every surface.

Sherry walked toward Gracie with a brown paper envelope, the nervous little dog at her heels. "Okay, here it is. I hope it helps you figure out what happened."

"I hope so, too. Thanks." Gracie dug in her purse and pulled out a business card. "Feel free to give me a call if you think of anything else."

As she came out of the apartment, she saw Tyler at the other end of the breezeway between apartments. His phone was at his ear, his head down, tension in every line of his body.

Gracie cleared her throat.

He spun around and, as he saw her, his face relaxed until a split second later when the anger set in. He muttered something into the phone and hung it up.

She walked toward him, though really, judging by the expression on his face, she thought it might be in her best interest to run for the car.

"Where were you?" Tyler didn't yell, but she could see it was an effort for him to hold back. Truth be told, the quiet, serious tone in his voice scared her more than if he'd been shouting.

"I was waiting for you to get here, and then I met Sherry, Daphne's neighbor. We got to talking—"

"And you just went into an apartment with someone you don't even know?" He wielded his hand like a blade, slicing it through the air as he gestured at the other apartment.

"If you'll let me explain—"

"There's nothing to explain. It was stupid." Gracie's spine snapped straight at those words. "And when I got here and saw your car in the parking lot and you were nowhere to be found, I thought something had happened to you."

The undisguised fear in his voice made her relent—a little.

"I was fine, Tyler. I *am* fine."

He scrubbed a frustrated hand through his hair, leaving it standing on end. "I know that. But you could have been hurt."

She took two hesitant steps forward and held out a hand, but he didn't take it. "I didn't think. I'm sorry."

As she let the hand drop, he reached for it, pressed a kiss to the tips of her fingers, then drew her closer and murmured against her hair, "You were right this morning."

Until now, her father's arms had been the only man's to wrap around her. She hadn't found a man she'd wanted to be that close to. Until now. Her pulse quickened as she wrapped her arms around him, too, feeling the hard strength in his back.

It was a lovely feeling, her heart fluttered and warmth rushed her, making her fingers tingle. But it wasn't a safe feeling, not at all.

She stepped back. Blinked. "What did you say?"

"You were right. And believe me, that's not an easy thing for me to admit. I won't lie to you or mislead you, Gracie. Not again."

Gracie took another step away from him. She couldn't breathe.

"You okay?"

She shook her head. He'd so totally rattled her. "No. I'm fine. Good. Let's go in. I got permission from the captain to visit the scene."

Tyler hesitated and then pulled a knife from his pocket and slit the seal on the door. He pushed it open. After one day, the small apartment smelled musty from being closed up, the organic scent of death mixing with old apartment.

In her bag, Gracie carried a digital video recorder, about the size of a deck of cards.

"I know the CSI team will have video, but if I'm asked to look at a scene, I usually take my own. It's sometimes useful when I want to look back later."

"What exactly do you look for?" He hadn't realized that she would go to crime scenes.

"There are things you can tell about a person from the crime they commit and the way they commit it. The space they live in holds clues, too."

"So you profile them?" He walked the perimeter of the room, looking for anything they might've missed yesterday.

"Not exactly profiling. I give my impression of the crime scene from a psychological perspective. It's a subtle difference, but still a difference."

She walked the edge of the room, filming, trying to capture every detail—from the creepy walls that sort of matched hers, to the sheets covering the furniture, to the bloodstain on the carpet that showed the position of the body. The police had taken the murder weapon, a heavy brass lamp base.

She stopped filming and looked around. "Why would she kill him in an apartment that she'd so carefully matched to mine?"

"She didn't plan to kill him." Tyler looked up from a drawer in the kitchen.

"Right. She also wouldn't have left the cat if she'd been thinking things through. Maybe he threatened her."

Tyler slammed the drawer shut. "I think he came to get payment and tell her he was off the case. He didn't bargain for all the police attention he's been getting."

"So, somehow he figured out where she was and followed her here?" Gracie clicked off the camera.

"Either that or she invited him here with the intention of somehow getting him to do what she wanted. He refused. So she killed him."

Gracie shook her head. "We're just guessing now. What do we know about her?"

"Lack of a father figure. History of drug abuse."

"Did you confirm that?"

He nodded. "I got a copy of a police report from Albuquerque. She was nineteen."

"I haven't seen any evidence here that she was using, but she might've been thinking clearly enough to take her stash with her, if she had one. She was thinking clearly enough to steal the victim's van." Gracie walked to the bedroom and switched the recorder back on.

"This is just too creepy, to be filming pictures of myself at a crime scene."

"What sticks out to me is that there's nothing of *her* here. It looks like an undercover crash pad."

She clicked the camera off again. "What do you mean?"

"You see what she wants you to see here. The apartment reflects the cover, not the real person—other than the pictures of you, and those she was studying. She's convinced herself that if she'd been you, her life would be great." He pulled open the closet door. She'd obviously taken the clothes, but there was a puddle of fabric on the floor. He picked it up. A swirly skirt, like those Gracie favored.

Gracie looked at it and fought back nausea. "I'm the cover."

"She's taking on your identity a little at a time. First the bank accounts, then Facebook. She posted to you, but she also posted as you. There's probably more that we haven't discovered yet. Did you check the bathroom?"

Gracie sucked in air. "Not yet."

She walked into the tiny space. Not surprisingly, she found her brand of shampoo in the shower. As she scanned with the video camera, she noted a box of black hair color by the sink. "Hey, Tyler, what do you make of that?"

"I have no idea. Maybe her hair was black before it was blond?" He walked back into the bedroom. "I don't like how fixated she is on you."

"The good thing is, from a psychological standpoint, she needs me right now." She didn't want to think about what would happen when Daphne didn't need her anymore. She pulled the small package from her purse. "The neighbor said this was delivered for Daphne today. Should we open it?"

He handed her his knife. She sliced into the package and poured the contents onto the bed. An ID set—driver's license, insurance card and police ID—fell out into a pile. All in Gracie's name. But the photo, like the apartment, was slightly skewed. Because the picture wasn't Gracie.

"We already knew she wanted your life." Tyler's voice was flat. "Now we know how far she's prepared to go to get it."

THIRTEEN

Gracie turned her little car toward the coffee shop on Beach Boulevard. Tyler had told her to go straight home. He'd called Joe Sheehan himself and ordered him to meet her at the estate. She'd called Joe back and made arrangements for him to meet her at Sip This instead. After a day like today, she needed comfort, and a cup of tea at Sailor Sloan's place had her name all over it.

The idea that she had to call a police officer to make a simple stop on her way home made her skin crawl.

She met Joe on the front steps of the old house-turned-coffee shop. "Hey, thanks for meeting me here. If you want coffee, I'm buying."

"I want coffee." The words were said in the tone usually reserved for fervent prayer.

Gracie laughed and pulled open the wide oak door. "Long night last night?"

"Yeah, we got a call-out right before the end of my shift. And I may be sleep and caffeine deprived, but I haven't forgotten why I'm here. You go first."

The shop was nearly empty, so Gracie leaned on the counter, while Joe found a table. He ran a hand over his shaved head and crossed his arms, looking mean.

Sailor Sloan jerked her head at Joe as she wiped the counter. "What's up with Muscles over there?"

"Joe is my escort for the evening. Tyler had Matt's wedding rehearsal tonight, and he didn't want me to be alone."

"I see." From the confused expression on her face, clearly, she didn't.

"I have a weird, um, family situation going on right now." Gracie opened her mouth to explain and then closed it again. "Let's just say I really need some tea. Oh, and Joe wants coffee."

Sailor took two mugs from under the counter. She filled one with steaming-hot coffee and slid it across to Gracie for Joe. "I saw you coming out of the bank yesterday. I hollered at you, but you didn't see me."

Gracie lifted Joe's cup to take it to him but stopped mid-motion. "I don't think that was me, sweetie."

"It was. You had on one of your cute little skirts."

Her stomach twisted as she imagined Daphne wearing the skirt they'd found in the bottom of the closet, pretending to be her. "What time was this?"

"Yesterday morning around eleven. I went to the bank after the morning coffee rush."

"Sailor, I was in court all morning yesterday. I was sitting in the witness box at eleven."

Hot water nearly overflowed the mug as Sailor stared at Gracie. Just in time, she let the lever go and the water flow stopped. "But you were—" Her shoulders drooped as she realized. "You weren't at the bank yesterday?"

Gracie shook her head.

Joe walked to the counter, snagged the mug with his coffee in it from Gracie's hand and took a swig. "Is there a problem, ladies?"

"Yes. Sailor thinks she saw me at the bank yesterday, but it wasn't me, it was—"

"Your crazy sister." At her look, he shrugged. "I was at the crime scene yesterday and Tyler filled me in. As it happens, I have a couple of crazy sisters. I think they're more like the shave-your-eyebrows-off-while-you-sleep variety of crazy than the murder-you-in-your-bed kind, but you never know."

Joe Sheehan had just uttered the most words he'd ever spoken to her at one time, despite the fact that they'd worked together for almost two years. He tipped his mug at her. "Everybody's got family, Gracie. Just because yours is a little more out there than most doesn't mean anything. Anybody that's got family's got dysfunction. It's all relative."

"You got that right." Sailor's brother was Cruse Conyers, the top cop. And not immune to family drama. She gave Gracie a sideways look and slid a couple of pieces of pie onto the granite counter. "On the house. You both look like you could use it."

Sailor walked away and Gracie took a bite of pie. She loved Sailor's baked goods, but thinking about everything going on turned the flaky goodness into dust in her mouth. She dropped the fork onto the plate and buried her head in her hands. "I wish I knew how to get in touch with her."

Joe had a jagged scar running from the corner of his left eye into his hairline. He rubbed it with a frown. "What would you tell her if you could?"

"To just stop. If I'd known she existed I would've welcomed her here. But she killed two people and—I think it's pretty clear she's going to try to kill me."

"We're not going to let her do that. Tyler's watching your back, and you've got the whole Sea Breeze Police Department on your side. You're ours, Gracie. We're not going to let anything happen to you."

Joe's phone rang. "Go for Sheehan."

As he listened, his face settled into serious lines. "Got it. We'll be right there."

He pressed END and turned to Gracie. "There's been an accident. Tyler's okay, but he had a blowout. That truck of his rolled when the tire blew. They've taken him to the hospital."

Gracie blew through the hospital doors like a tornado. If Tyler hadn't seen the fear on her face, he would've laughed. "Gracie, over here."

He was sitting on a gurney in a curtained area.

She came to a stop just outside the opening, spotting blood all over his white shirt. "It's bad, isn't it? You look bad."

"It looks worse than it is. Come on in." He

motioned to the one chair in the little cubicle, but she gripped his hand instead.

Her eyes were big and worried. "It looks like you've been in a slasher film. What happened?"

He shifted the ice bag on his forehead. "The tire blew. I tried to keep it on the road, but the shift in balance was too much for my truck at the speed I was going..." Joe appeared in the doorway of the curtained area "...which definitely wasn't speeding, Detective Sheehan."

"You were lucky. They pulled a spike out of your left front tire."

"Something I picked up on the road?"

Joe shrugged. "There was also one in the left rear tire."

"Daphne did this. She said on Facebook that she would come after people I care about. She said she would take away things that are important to me one by one. She said that, Joe." Her voice was climbing.

"Okay, Gracie. We need to think about how to keep you safe. And since Tyler's been helping you with the investigation, obviously that makes him a target, too."

The nurse came in with paperwork. Joe and Gracie stepped out. "All right, Mr. Clark, you're set to go. Your mother says you should know how to take care of stitches, since you had them often enough as a kid."

It was great having a mother who was also the administrator of the hospital. "Yes, ma'am. I think I've got it covered."

She handed him a set of scrubs. "If you'd like to change."

"Thank you." He left his jeans on but stripped off the bloody shirt.

So, the question was, what to do with Gracie? It had gone past the point of staying in the main house while she stayed in the pool house. They needed a new plan.

He would suggest his condo, but there was no guarantee that Gracie's sister didn't already know where it was.

His mom walked through the curtain. "Well, you certainly know how to liven up a party."

"You shouldn't be here, Mom."

"Well, after Matthew came in with a concussion last year and I didn't know it until after the fact, I might have yelled a little. I don't think any child of mine will ever be in the ER again without me knowing about it."

"I'm fine, Mom."

"I know, baby." She brushed his hair away from the cut on his forehead. "You're going to look pretty in the wedding pictures."

He made a face. "Nice."

"Bring Gracie to stay at our house. There'll be lots of activity going on. It's not like anyone will even notice we've added two more people." She sighed. "Besides, the way your father's acting, we'll probably need counseling before the weekend is over."

He snorted a laugh. "I love you, Mom."

"Love you back. I'll see you at home." She breezed out the same way she came in.

Tyler walked out behind her and found Gracie pacing the waiting room, chewing one pink-tipped fingernail. Joe sat in a chair, his eyes following her as she went from one side of the room to the other.

Tyler leaned against a pillar, waiting for Gracie to come back his way. "So, you ready to get out of here?"

She stopped in front of him. "Yes. Are you okay?"

"Perfect."

"Sure you are. I'm driving."

They walked out the door of the ER, Joe behind them. A tan FWC Law Enforcement truck with a bar of blue lights pulled up under the portico.

Ethan rolled down the window. "We've been brothers a long time, and you've gotten me in all kinds of trouble, but if you ever send me on a mission like that again, our relationship is over."

Tyler looked in the window and saw the cat carrier. He didn't think the cat was quite as happy to see him. One claw poked through the metal screen and held on.

"Is that Charlemagne?" Gracie nudged Tyler out of the way and opened the door. "Poor kitty, he's had a rough couple of days. Thanks for getting him, Ethan, but I'm not sure I understand why you did."

Ethan raised an eyebrow at Tyler. Out of the corner of her eye, she saw Joe walk away, his hands in his pockets.

"We'll be safer if we stay at Mom and Dad's. There will be lots of people around. Less chance of something happening."

"You don't think I'll put them in danger by being there? What about Marcus?"

"They'll be fine. Between me and Matt and my dad, you'll have three law enforcement officers on the property with you. If Ethan will stay, we'll have four."

"Someone will have to get my dress for the wedding."

Ethan put the car in gear and let it roll forward. "Don't look at me. I got the cat."

Joe raised his hand. "I'll get a black-and-white to meet me there. Is it going to be hard for me to find?"

"No, it's all in one place, right by my closet door."

"All right, I'll meet you at Tyler's parents'. Stay safe."

Staying safe was exactly what Tyler intended. If someone wanted to get to Gracie, they were going to have to go through him first.

Gracie woke with a start. A strange noise was coming from the kitchen area. She threw a robe on over her PJs and peeked through the hall door. Tyler stood at the kitchen counter in sweats and a T-shirt chopping…something.

She looked at her watch. Three a.m.

Maybe he had a headache and couldn't sleep. Or maybe something was bothering him. She looked down the long, dark hall at the closed doors. She tightened the belt on her robe and padded into the kitchen.

She leaned against the counter next to him as he worked with butter and flour in a big silver bowl. "Hey."

"Hey yourself."

"You making biscuits?" she asked.

"Yep."

"Do you always get up at three in the morning?"

He looked at her and she could see that his eyes were tired. "Do you always ask so many questions?"

She hopped up to sit on the counter beside where he was working. "Don't you know me by now?"

"You do have a point." Tyler added buttermilk and eggs to the crumb mixture.

She knew that he wouldn't be up in the middle of the night cooking for no reason. Which meant that he was worried about her situation. Or... "Nightmares?"

He stopped mixing. "What is it with you? It's freaky the way you read minds."

"I don't read minds. It's pretty logical after everything you've been through that there would be some lasting effects. Nightmares, flashbacks. Insomnia. Sound familiar?"

He added some cheddar cheese to the mixture and turned it out onto a surface he had prepared. "Maybe."

"What are you doing? Don't you have to knead that or something?"

"No, you don't want to over-mix it or the dough will be tough. You just shape it."

He patted the dough into a one-inch-thick square.

"Do you want to talk about what's keeping you up at night?"

The lights were out except in the kitchen, and the rest of the house, despite being full of people, was dark and silent. Tyler cut a biscuit and put it on the prepared pan. "Sometimes I just don't know where to go from here."

He cut until he got to the last little bit of dough. Tossing the leftovers into the garbage can, he shrugged, like, *You asked.*

"I think starting over is really hard, to rebuild yourself into something different than you imagined that you would be. But I think you have a lot to work with, Tyler. You might not be able to see that clearly because of all that you've been through, but I can see it."

He stared down at the pan of biscuits, his hands gripping the handles on either side of the pan. "You asked me one time if I crossed the line. The real answer is—I'm not sure. At the time I thought I was doing what I had to do, but now I don't know. Things look different on the outside."

"Sometimes even when you do the right thing for the right reason it doesn't feel right?"

His eyes shot up to meet hers. "Yeah. Except in this case, I nearly let someone die just so I wouldn't jeopardize the case. She survived, but it was because my brother risked his own life to save hers."

Ahh. "Tyler, it's easy to look back now and think that you should've done things differently. Let's assume that you made the wrong decision—"

"I made the wrong decision, Gracie. There's no assumption about it." He opened the oven and shoved the pan of biscuits in.

"Okay. You made the wrong choice. Now what?"

"What do you mean, '*now what?*'" He spun around to face her but didn't come any closer.

"I mean, where do you go from here? Do you live your life in shame because you made a mistake?"

"Maybe I should."

He was killing her. She wanted to go to him, give him comfort. But she knew he wouldn't accept it, not now. "You have to learn how to forgive yourself. Because until you can, all these things that you're doing are only masking the problem, not making it go away. You can't find a new life until you can let the old one go."

"That's easy for you to say, isn't it? But how good are you at letting go of the past?"

He was smart, she'd give him that. She did have to come to grips with her history. Her past was stalking her in an extremely real and present way. His was stalking him too, just much more insidiously.

She slid off the counter and went to the refrigerator for a drink. "Deflecting the point to me, while valid, does not make this any less about you and what you have to do if you want to be healthy."

"Now you sound like a shrink." He sat down at the kitchen table and picked at a piece of cake that someone had left sitting there earlier.

She popped the top on a diet soda and took a sip, giving herself a minute to collect her thoughts. She recognized that he was trying to get a rise out of her. It was humbling to also realize that maybe she'd turned to professional jargon because he'd gotten a mite too close.

Gracie dropped into a kitchen chair. "We could turn this conversation to me, because you're right. I need to work on forgiveness and acceptance, but I wasn't the one up at three a.m. making biscuits."

He almost smiled. She saw it flicker in his eyes but then he nodded. "Yeah, but—" He stopped. "You're right as well. I could point the finger at you all night, but it wouldn't help either of us."

His hand clenched, but he shook it off. "I didn't know what it would mean when I signed on to the DEA. How much I would lose of myself when I agreed to go undercover. What there is left…I don't know, Gracie."

"Does it count that you risked your life to bring those guys down, Tyler? How many lives did you save because those drugs aren't on the streets anymore?"

"It helps. But that can't be all there is for me. Not anymore."

Gracie put her hand out on the table where he could reach it if he wanted to. "It's not all there is for you. It's not all there is to you. And you don't have to do this alone."

Tyler didn't move, but he gave a slight nod, his lips tight.

She'd said all she could. The rest was up to him. And they both needed some sleep. The timer on the oven beeped. She started to walk away.

He grabbed her hand, held on. "Thank you."

As she walked down the shadowy hall toward her guest bedroom, she thought about Tyler. She saw men like him every day. Men who had given every part of themselves to keep others safe. Who'd risked their lives in every sense of the word.

Who would stand with them? God knew they needed someone on their side.

Matt and Lara's reception was held in an old restored firehouse in downtown Pensacola. The building boasted nearly floor-to-ceiling windows and exposed brick walls. Huge brass chandeliers hung from the ceiling. Gracie wanted to take it all in, from the ancient fire truck, where Matt and Lara were currently having their picture taken, to the cake, center stage in the room. The two had chosen not to serve dinner at the reception, but waiters circulated the room carrying trays of heavy hors d'oeuvres.

"It's absolutely stunning," she murmured. "Perfect for Matt and Lara."

"You look stunning."

She looked up at his words, but Tyler wasn't looking at her, instead studying the cake creation in the center of the room.

"You clean up pretty nice, yourself. Do

you do this often?" As she spoke, the DJ announced that the bride and groom would like for their guests to join them on the dance floor for their first dance.

Instead of answering her question, Tyler swung her onto the dance floor. She laughed, the feeling in her chest giddy little bubbles. He whirled her around and, as the music changed, his arms closed around her, drawing her into his embrace.

She closed her eyes, letting herself experience the moment. She had feelings for Tyler. It wasn't any astounding revelation, really. She'd been drawn to him from the beginning, even when she'd suspected that there was more to him than he was sharing.

She'd been right. For the reasons she thought then, but for so much more. He had so much depth, so much capacity for good, so much he wanted to give to his family and friends.

His arm around her back felt warm and strong.

What did it feel like to fall for someone?

Did it feel like sailing in the middle of the ocean, wind in your face, wild abandon?

Because that's what it felt like at this very moment.

She'd been careful for so long. She'd waited.

And waited and waited. Maybe it was time to feel the wind in her face. She chuckled.

Tyler leaned back so he could see her expression. "What's funny?"

His dark brown eyes were liquid chocolate, reflecting the glimmer of candles and the gleam of the brass in the room. She realized as she looked into them that she wanted the opportunity to get to know him better. To really find out if there could be something between them.

But she didn't say that. Instead, she risked laying out an idea that had begun as a tiny seed when Tyler served her breakfast on the patio. "I'm thinking we should turn the big house into a bed and breakfast."

"We?"

"You don't think I could run a B&B alone, do you? The only thing I know how to do in the kitchen is open cans."

Instead of answering, he eased them to the edge of the dance floor and grabbed two glasses of water from a passing waiter.

She took a sip of the icy water, to hide that her fingers were trembling. She'd been making plans, assuming that he'd want to stay in her life. And chances were he'd already been making plans of his own.

Her feelings shouldn't even have been bruised. Her father had taught her at an early age about plans being broken. "You know what? You shouldn't answer that. I know you have a lot to think about right now."

His eyes followed the progress of the bride and groom as they made their way across the dance floor to the cake. "I never wanted to be a cop. 'We're a cop family,' my dad used to say. I think he wanted all of us to work for the Sheriff's Department."

"What he wanted was for you boys to be happy and productive," Reed Clark said, as he walked up behind them.

Every muscle in Tyler's body tensed. "Really, Dad? Because what I remember is saying that I wanted to take some time off after college to decide where I wanted to go and you hitting the roof."

"Of course I hit the roof. You wanted to backpack around the country taking pictures. You'd never even owned a camera. You could've worked as a deputy and supported yourself while you decided what to be."

"If that's true, then why did you give Matt such a hard time?"

"Oh, that. Cops always pick on firefighters. Firefighters always pick on cops. Cops win."

He said the last loud enough for the firefighters at the next table to overhear.

Matt's partner, True, backed into their conversation. "Watch out, sir. You know what they say…if you can't take the heat, become a cop."

Another joined in. "If firefighting was easy…" He looked back at the table of firefighters in their dress blues.

"…cops would do it," they chorused.

Tyler forced a laugh, but Gracie could tell that he was weighing whether what his father said was the truth. It seemed like maybe they both had an image of their father that wasn't quite reality.

"I'm proud of you, Tyler. You did a hard job well. And whatever you choose to do now, I'll still be proud of you."

"Maybe Marcus will go to work for the Sheriff's Department," Gracie put in.

"Heaven help us all if someone lets Marcus carry a gun." Reed looked at his youngest son in the center of the dance floor, where he tucked one foot behind the other knee, dipped to the floor, then stood and spun around, all in one smooth move. Reed shook his head. "He's definitely adopted. You never had moves like that."

"What are you talking about?" Tyler grinned at his father and joined his brother on the dance floor, executing a complicated move of his own that had his dad shaking his head once again.

"Boys. I was lucky enough to have four of 'em. Now I'm going to dance with my wife." Reed started toward Bethanne, but not before Gracie heard him say again, half under his breath, "Truly lucky."

Someone bumped into her from behind, nearly sending her sprawling. "'Scuse me."

"No problem," Gracie glanced back, but the person was already gone.

Matt and Lara had made it to the center of the room, where the beautiful white-on-white wedding cake stood. All eyes were on them as he cut the first piece and laughed as he pantomimed smashing it in her face.

"Just remember I get to go next, *honey*." Lara's serene smile didn't hide the mischievous spark in her eye.

Matt allowed Lara to gracefully take the first bite from him and then pulled her in for a dramatic kiss. Behind her, the firefighters from Station One yelled and stomped their feet.

Matt let Lara loose with a flourish, leaving

her to fan herself, just before she crammed a huge piece of cake in his mouth. The crew of firefighters behind Gracie hooted again, fists pumping in the air.

Marcus appeared at her elbow. "I brought you some punch."

"Thanks. Want to sit down?" Gracie had rarely seen Marcus without a mischievous expression on his face and a twinkle of trouble in his eyes, but this afternoon his expression was serious. He pulled the chair out for her and her heart melted. "You look like you've got something on your mind. Wanna share?"

"Not really." He took a swig of his punch and watched Tyler swing his mom around the dance floor. "Tyler's pretty cool. I didn't much like him before because it made Mom sad to talk about him. But he's okay."

She nodded, wondering whether she should keep poking around. "I like Tyler, too."

He nodded, very man-like. "Figured you did. He's been hanging out at your place."

"He's staying in a different house than I am."

Marcus seemed to take that in stride. He took another swig of the super-sweet punch and she wondered how good that could be for his diabetes. "My mother used to have guys stay over."

Gracie stared at him a second before realizing he was talking about his biological mother. She nodded. "I bet that was hard for you."

He shrugged. "I was only seven when they took me away."

She wanted to be careful that she didn't say anything hurtful. He had a new family he loved, but this was his mother he was talking about. "I guess that was hard for you."

"We didn't have much to eat. When I came to live with the Clarks, Mom let me have a basket of snacks that I could pick from whenever I wanted. I slept with it for a while. Guess that sounds pretty lame."

"It sounds logical to me." She chewed the corner of her bottom lip for a second, thinking how to phrase the next question. "So being with the Clarks makes you happy?"

His eyes suddenly brimmed with tears, much like the other day at the coffee shop, but he whispered, "Is it wrong? That I love my Mom so much that I never want to go back to my old family?"

Her heart felt like it was breaking into tiny pieces. "No, bud. It's normal that you would feel that way. Bethanne is your real mom. She adopted you because she loves you with all her heart—the way a mother is supposed to love her kids."

Marcus jumped to his feet and hugged her, so tight that her eyes watered. "Thanks, Doc, that's what I thought. I'm going for cake. Want some?"

She grinned at the rapid mood change because that was the Marcus she'd gotten to know. "You go ahead. I'll get some in a bit." He was gone before she finished her sentence.

It was impossible to know without all the paperwork and follow-up interviews whether Marcus's biological mother had truly loved him. Even if she did, the truth was that parents didn't always do the right thing.

Her dad hadn't done the right thing by lying to her all those years. Tyler's dad hadn't always said the right things or let his boys feel his unconditional love. Marcus's mother had let him go after he'd experienced things that no seven-year-old should experience. But there was another truth, and that was that they each had a heavenly Father whose love made up for the lack of a perfect earthly parent.

And maybe Marcus would never know the truth about his biological mother, but he would have the benefit of knowing that he had a family who loved him.

Minutes later, Tyler walked up. "Seen Marcus? Mom wants a picture of all of us in our tuxedos by the fire truck while Ethan's still here. He's getting that panicky look on his face, like in another minute he'll bolt."

"Marcus was here talking to me about two minutes ago. He went to get a piece of cake. I figured he got side-tracked."

"Mom said he needs to check his blood sugar. There's way too much temptation around here."

Tyler didn't panic, not yet, but he didn't have a good feeling. In fact, he had an itchy feeling between his shoulder blades that said, *Things are not right.*

He turned around and filled in the group of firefighters sitting at the table behind her. "It's probably nothing, but we can't find Marcus. Can you spread out and help us look?"

As the firefighters started searching the building, Tyler pushed open the huge front doors that opened onto the street. There were people outside—a few smokers and at least one couple who'd come out for some quiet conversation.

"Tyler." Gracie followed him outside, her

deep blue eyes terrified in the dim light of the downtown street lamps. "I keep seeing that Facebook status she posted on my profile. It wouldn't take a genius to know Marcus is special to us."

"We're going to find him." He wouldn't allow any other thought to enter his mind. They would find him. The thought crept in anyway... *Would they find him in time?*

FOURTEEN

Tyler's long legs ate up the pavement as he searched the perimeter of the building, even looking between the Dumpsters. Gracie's heels clacked behind him as she followed, keeping an eye out for anything he missed.

When they were back where they started, Tyler approached the group standing by the door. Some of them were the same ones who'd been there when he and Gracie first came out. "Did anyone see a kid come through here not too long ago, maybe fifteen minutes?" he asked.

They looked at each other and then at Gracie. Finally the guy sitting to the side with his date said, "Yeah, I did. He was dressed in a tuxedo and he was with her."

He pointed at Gracie, whose face crumpled in distress.

"Can you tell me if they left in a car, or if they were walking?"

The woman with him answered, "I think they were in a car. They went toward the parking lot. I wasn't really paying attention."

"Thanks." Tyler grabbed Gracie by the hand, dragging her along with him. "I want you to stay with my dad. I'm going to go look for them."

"No." She slowed to a crawl, every muscle pulling against him. "I have to go. This is my fault."

It wasn't her fault, not by a long shot, but he didn't have time to argue with her. "I'm not going to stop you, but I think this is a bad idea."

He switched direction and went back toward the parking lot, stopping only to talk to Matt's partner, True. "We found a witness that saw him leave with someone who looked like Gracie. Keep looking here, just in case, and call me if you find anything. I'll do the same."

True nodded. "Are you going to bring in the SBPD?"

"Yes. I'll call it in." Tyler pushed through the door to the parking lot, fear for his little brother coursing through him. Regardless of what he'd told Gracie, Daphne had already killed twice, and he didn't think she would hesitate to kill again.

Marcus was a pawn in her plan.

"Where do you think she'll take him?" Gracie clicked the seat belt as he slammed the truck into gear and sped out of the parking lot.

"I only have one guess, and I'm praying I'm right." Otherwise, Marcus would be in trouble.

"I think I know a way we could be sure. Wouldn't Marcus have his cell phone?"

He slowed the car as his head whipped toward hers. "Always. And my mom has that 'locator' thing. My brothers and I were talking about how lucky it was that didn't exist when we were teenagers."

Tyler flipped the lights off and pulled to the side of the road near the long driveway leading to Gracie's home. The moon, round and full in the sky, lent just enough illumination to see.

He pulled his laptop out of the backseat and pulled up the website for the cell company. When the prompt came up, he typed in his mother's cell number.

"Won't you need a password?"

"Yes, but my mother always uses the same

one, God love her." He typed in the name of the street where his mother grew up and clicked on the GPS icon for Marcus's phone.

He glanced at Gracie. She had her eyes closed, her lips moving in a silent prayer for Marcus's safety.

"There." He zoomed in on the spot with the mouse and pointed. "They're here. I'll walk in. I really think you should wait in the car for the police."

He opened the driver's-side door as Gracie opened the other side and slid to the ground.

"There is zero chance that I will stay in the car." In her evening bag, her cell phone buzzed. She fumbled for it, finding it in the very bottom. "Gracie VanDoren."

Tyler reached under the seat. Somewhere under there was his big flashlight.

She covered the mouthpiece. "Alarm company. The silent alarm in the main house was tripped. Should I tell them to send the police?"

He started to shake his head, no. "We need backup but—"

Gracie held a finger up to silence him. "No, we're in contact with the police ourselves." She listened and then said, "Okay, thanks, I appreciate it."

She pushed the END button. "I'll call Cruse and let him know what's going on. We're going to need help, but it's going to be tricky. They won't be able to come in lights flashing and sirens blaring or we'll risk Marcus."

"Okay, good idea." Hyperaware of the time ticking by, and sick, really sick, at the idea of his little brother being held by a deranged woman, Tyler opened the lock box on the back of his truck. He pulled out two semiautomatics and extra ammunition as Gracie hung up. "Are you weapons qualified?"

"Yes, but I haven't carried in this type of situation."

"Okay, no problem." If they needed a backup, he'd have it. And if she needed it, Gracie would have a weapon. "Look in the glove compartment. I think there's another little flashlight in there."

He took off his tie, started to shed his tuxedo coat, but thought better of it. Nothing like being a huge, glowing, white target in a dark house.

Gracie handed him the flashlight.

"You carry the big one. Use it as a weapon if you need to." He checked the load on one of the guns and tucked it into the small of his back. He checked the one he would carry, too. "There's a light on in the pool house."

"I left that one on." She took a deep breath. "Okay, so this is all about what she missed, about what she feels should've been hers. I think she'll be in the bedroom I used growing up."

"Good call. I don't see any lights on in the main house, but we'll check there first. We'll go in the back door by the kitchen. Got the keys, just in case?"

She held them up.

"Okay, we're set." The palm trees Gracie's dad had planted cast long, swaying shadows across the driveway. And there, as one of the shadows shifted, he caught a glimpse of something shiny in the bushes. A car was parked in the wooded area to the left of the driveway— another few feet and he'd have missed it.

The car was a little black compact he'd never seen before. He thumbed the tag number into a text message and noted the sticker on the back window. It was a rental. He had no idea if his source would be able to get back to him in time, but they needed all the information they could get.

As they got closer to the house, he realized they definitely weren't going to need a key. It looked like the door had been pried open with a crowbar.

At the sound of tires on gravel, Gracie put her hand on Tyler's back. No lights, no siren, but it was a police cruiser. Whoever it was must've been very close when the call went out.

Joe Sheehan stepped out of the car and met them at the base of the stairs. He wore a bullet-resistant vest over jeans and a black T-shirt.

His eyes on Tyler's weapon, he said, "You're planning to go in?"

"My little brother's inside."

Joe nodded but said, "We should wait for backup. We can clear the house much faster with help."

"I can't wait. Marcus needs insulin as soon as possible. I have it in my pocket."

Joe weighed this revelation with his usual calm. "All right. I'll go in with you."

"I don't want to leave her outside alone." Tyler looked at Gracie. He didn't want her here at all.

"I'll wait here while you clear the kitchen and then I'll stand right inside the door and wait for the cavalry."

When he hesitated, she said, "I'll be fine."

He reached around and pulled the spare

weapon from the small of his back, placing it in her palm. "Keep this. We don't know what she's up to."

"Go. Find Marcus."

Before he could think about it, he gave her a quick, hard hug. Just as quick, he released her and disappeared into the house behind Joe.

Gracie paced the length of the marble-tiled patio and tried not to worry. Pragmatically, she knew that worrying did no good. Realistically, she was terrified that Daphne had already done something to Marcus.

So she prayed. That Marcus's blood sugar would miraculously level out. That Daphne would think this through. That Tyler and Joe would be safe.

And, as she eased through the kitchen door, she prayed that she could accept that her dad hadn't hurt her on purpose. He couldn't have known that what he did would have such a profound effect on his two daughters.

She fingered the purity ring on the chain around her neck. She'd needed it when he'd given it to her. Needed the reminder, the standard to cling to. In the end, it hadn't been about what her dad believed, but about what she chose to believe for herself.

Maybe choosing not to date wasn't the right

choice for everyone, but it had been the right choice for her. To wait until she knew what she wanted. Until she found a man worth waiting for, worth loving. A man like Tyler.

What was going on? It was deathly quiet upstairs.

Behind her she heard the snick of a gun being cocked. She froze.

"Don't move. Put the gun on the ground."

An older female voice, not Daphne. Sheriff's Department, maybe? She raised her hands, letting Tyler's weapon dangle from her thumb. "I'm Gracie VanDoren. I own this house."

"I know who you are. Put the gun on the ground and kick it to me."

She turned to face the woman and found herself staring at the double barrel of a sawed-off shotgun. This was no cop. Slowly, she raised her eyes. She sucked in her breath. *"Regina?"*

"Gun on the ground and kick it back to me."

Gracie bent her knees and placed the gun on the floor of the kitchen, her stomach roiling. She kicked the gun toward Daphne's mother. "What are you doing here?"

"Enough with the questions. Let's go. We're going through the yard to the garden shed."

Apparently she'd guessed wrong and sent Tyler and Joe on a needless mission. But having Regina in the mix changed the dynamics. The raw edges of the shotgun poked her in the back as if to demonstrate that point.

She raised her hands again where Regina could see them, wordlessly saying, *Fine, I'm cooperating.*

The shed sat at the edge of the gardens, almost out of sight of the main house, near the gazebo, where Gracie and her mom used to sit and tell stories. Sometimes after work, her dad would join them until the sun went down and the three of them would reluctantly return to the house.

She hadn't thought of those times for years. And with that memory, Gracie realized she'd been wrong. Her father hadn't been unhappy. He'd loved Gracie's mother. He'd loved Gracie.

She could forgive him for keeping his secret, for wanting to keep his life with Regina and Daphne separate. She didn't understand it, but she could forgive it and let the past stay in the past.

Except for part of that past was poking her in the back with a gun right now. "Is Marcus all right?"

"Shut up." Regina pushed her from behind and Gracie stumbled, scraping her knees on the stone path.

"We told you what would happen if you didn't stop investigating."

We? How long had Regina been working with Daphne? Since before they came to visit her in Arizona? She pushed back to her feet, the questions tumbling in her mind one after the other, questions she didn't dare ask.

There had to be a reason she was still alive. And if there was something they wanted from her, maybe she could use that to get information about Marcus.

Tyler would find them. Gracie just prayed he wouldn't be too late.

"Joe, look." As they reached the top of the stairs, Tyler caught a glimpse through the huge picture window of two shadows moving across the yard, one with blond ringlets gleaming in the moonlight. "Two people just went into the garden shed."

"Gracie?"

"I saw blond hair." Tyler's stomach knotted. He should've made her stay at the reception. As if he could've.

"Blonde could be the sister."

"You're right." It was possible that Marcus

had just been used as bait to get Gracie here. The danger level for both of them had just skyrocketed.

"We need to check it out." Joe started down the stairs. "You can back me up."

"Let's check the rest of the upstairs for Marcus. And then you can back *me* up."

"You're funny for an ex-fed." Joe quickly cleared the rooms on the left side of the hall while Tyler cleared the rooms on the right, along with the master bedroom at the end of the hall. "Nothing here."

"Nothing here either, but she was here." Tyler held up a princess crown made of paper that had been on the keepsake shelf with Gracie's childhood books. It was just the kind of thing that Daphne would zone in on. "I found it on the dressing table."

He started down the stairs. He held out a small hope that Gracie hadn't been captured, but the kitchen was empty. She wasn't there, but the handgun he'd given her to protect herself was on the floor.

She wouldn't have left it willingly. He picked it up, shoved it into his waistband and turned to Joe. "Text Cruse. Tell him they're on the grounds somewhere. To wait for word before moving."

And he prayed with those rusty skills that seemed to be getting a workout lately. *Dear God, please protect Gracie. She's a very special woman.* He swallowed hard. *Very special to me. Please, God.*

Regina pushed Gracie into the garden shed. The size of a small barn, it housed the tractor used to mow the lawn and the equipment for cleaning the pool.

She didn't turn on a light, but as Gracie's eyes adjusted to the dark room, she could see Marcus's dim shape, bound, lying against the far wall. His dark eyes blinked at her, but his mouth was covered with duct tape so he couldn't cry out.

She started toward him.

"Don't." The word cracked through the room.

"You would let him die?"

"I don't care if he lives or dies. I care that you give me the name of your father's accountant and how to get in touch with him."

"Why?" Gracie probed.

"Daphne becomes Gracie. She has your money and control over your father's estate. Daphne ceases to exist." Regina said it like a kindergarten teacher with a very slow student.

"No more Daphne." The words came from the darkest corner of the room.

"Daphne?" Gracie's breath rushed out with a gasp.

A woman stepped out of the shadows into a tiny crevice of light coming from the outside, lighting her hair and face. This was Gracie's sister. Her father's flesh and blood.

Gracie had wanted to see Daphne ever since she found out about her. Maybe it was morbid curiosity, but she leaned closer. They had a similar body type and their features were alike enough that she could see how people would mistake Daphne for her from a distance. "We really do look alike."

Daphne blinked and raised her clasped hands, which Gracie suddenly realized held a handgun. "Stop talking, Gracie. You're going to die. She's going to die, right, Mom? And I get everything that should've been mine all along."

"Shut up, Daphne." Regina waved her back, but Daphne only stepped forward, seemingly as fascinated by Gracie's face as Gracie was by hers.

Gracie didn't move—she wanted to see who was calling the shots here, though it seemed obvious at this point. "Why do you hate me,

Daphne? I didn't even know you existed until a few days ago."

"Liar. I knew about you." Her hands were shaking, the gun wavering wildly, the look in her eyes unfettered adrenaline as she reached with one hand to touch Gracie's blond curls.

"Do you know how I found out about you?" Gracie fought hard to maintain rational thought, but she was having a hard time putting herself in the role of psychologist when there was so much at stake.

"Your father told you."

"Daphne." Her mother's voice warned her off this subject.

"No. My father didn't tell me about you." *Calm, Gracie. Keep your voice level.* "I found out from someone I work with. You left DNA behind when you tried to blow up the big house. Why did you do that? If you wanted the house, why would you try to destroy it?"

"If I can't have it, you shouldn't have it either." She stepped away from Gracie, her eyes growing cold.

"You weren't thinking, Daphne. But now you know better." Regina's voice was hard, shoring up her partner in this game she was running. And it was becoming more and more clear who was running whom. Who wanted revenge and who was in it for the money. "We're going to live in the house that should've been ours all along."

And she must've come here to check on Daphne. When she saw just how much Daphne looked like Gracie, the idea came to her to switch their identities and keep the fortune for herself.

Or maybe it had been the plan all along and she'd totally taken them in. Which seemed more likely, given her comments.

Gracie took a deep breath and reminded herself not to get distracted. She needed to try to reach Daphne.

"There's no reason why we both shouldn't have the money and the properties, Daphne. He was a father to both of us. And now that I know about you, why wouldn't I share the inheritance with you?"

Daphne tilted her head. "You wouldn't do that." But there was a question in her voice.

"No, she wouldn't." Regina walked to Gracie, put the shotgun barrel in her chest and shoved her to the floor. "She's going to die, Daphne, and you're going to become Gracie. You're going to have everything you ever dreamed of. Everything she robbed you of as a child."

Gracie shivered. Regina talked about it so callously. It was a done deal in her mind. Her death meant nothing to Regina.

She thought about the request for her father's accountant. She'd removed all the financials from her father's office. They wouldn't be able to get into the pool house, not with the new security that Nolan Russ had put in. Even if they had, the accountant was only listed as a name, not a company.

Regina wouldn't be able to figure out that he was the one with the keys to the fortune, unless Gracie's father had told her.

Regina's end goal was so obvious now. She wasn't so sure about Daphne. Daphne seemed to be lost. Wanting connection with a family she'd never really known.

Gracie didn't care about the money, but she had to stall.

If she gave Regina the information she wanted, she and Marcus would both be dead within minutes.

Tyler made a wide circle around the shed. There were windows, but he couldn't see inside, other than vague shadows. He knew Gracie was inside that building. Possibly Marcus, too.

His phone vibrated in his coat pocket. He

pulled it out and checked the readout. His source. The rental car was registered to *Regina Graham?* Daphne's mother? What was she doing here?

Now for the big question—was she here to stop Daphne or help her?

Joe motioned to Tyler that he was going to the other side of the shed, where there was a door to a closet that ran the length of the building.

It was all Tyler could do not to storm the building. But he had to be smarter than that. There was no sound, none at all, except for the soft waves of the bay sliding into the shore. No light inside either, but as he circled he could see—barely—a woman standing in the middle of the room. Daphne?

Beside her stood Regina with a sawed-off shotgun.

So they were partners. That explained why Daphne switched cars after killing the P.I. Resentment burned in his gut. With everything in him, he wanted to kick down the door and bring Gracie out. He couldn't stand knowing that he was this close and couldn't get to her.

Tyler's stomach clenched. He recognized fear, had felt it often enough, but never for someone he cared about. Never for someone he loved.

And there it was. He loved Gracie.

She'd brought sunshine into his life and shown him that it was okay to be the person he'd always wanted to be. She was beautiful inside and out.

And he had no doubt that Daphne and Regina would kill her and Marcus.

They'd killed at least twice that he knew of and wouldn't hesitate to do it again. He was sweating, despite the chill in the air. Swiping his hand across his mouth, he reminded himself that Gracie was alive, and now he had something they hadn't had before. He knew where their hostages were.

Now he needed to figure out how to get them out.

FIFTEEN

Gracie eased backward on the floor a few inches closer to Marcus. Regina didn't seem to notice.

She was peering out the window. "Where are they?"

"Where are who?" Daphne twirled one of her look-alike curls on her finger.

"The cops. The big house had an alarm system. The cops should be here by now." Regina turned on Gracie. "You give me the name of the accountant or I shoot the kid."

Gracie took a deep breath. "I don't have it."

Regina slapped the back of her hand across Gracie's cheek. "Do you really think I'm so stupid that you can lie and get away with it? It was the accountant who told you how to find me in Arizona."

She lifted Marcus by the collar of his tux

shirt and shoved the shotgun under his chin. His eyes were wide and terrified. "Tell me."

"Don't hurt him." She closed her eyes. "It wasn't the accountant. I found out about you through the attorney for my father's estate." She froze because as soon as the words left her mouth, she knew she'd made a mistake.

The attorney would know the accountant's name. And Regina already knew who the attorney was because there had been a settlement made to her from the estate. Gracie had just made herself dispensable.

Slowly, Regina lifted the gun toward Gracie, the knowledge of the insane act she was about to commit lighting her eyes. Gracie scrambled away from her, crab-walking backward. "Wait. Regina, you don't need the attorney. You can end this tonight. I'll give you the name and number, but I don't have it on me. I have to get it from my house."

"Don't lie to me."

"I'm not. It's not listed as an accounting firm. He's a family friend, but I'll have to find the number." She looked from Regina to Daphne. "You'll have everything you want. *Everything.*"

Regina lowered the shotgun. Gracie breathed a silent sigh of relief. She'd bought some time.

But had she bought enough time for Tyler to find and rescue them before Regina killed them both?

Daphne wrapped duct tape around Gracie's wrists. "I'm sorry," she whispered into Gracie's ear. "I didn't want to hurt anyone. I just wanted what I didn't have. What I deserved to have."

Gracie thought fast. Turning Daphne against her mother would be difficult if not impossible, but maybe she could earn some second thoughts. "I always wanted a sister. I hated being an only child."

"Shut up, Gracie." Regina jerked Marcus to his feet. He swayed, his eyes rolling back into his head.

Gracie ignored her. "Daphne's a beautiful name. It sounds much better with VanDoren than Gracie."

Daphne stopped and looked at Gracie. The light in the shed was very dim, but Gracie could see the hurt in her sister's gray-blue eyes. "Your name isn't Gracie, it's Graciela. You're named after our great-grandmother."

"That's true. Where does Daphne come from?"

"My mother named me after the author of a book she was reading. I was named after a

writer. Not a grandmother. She's ready, Mom."
Daphne pulled a piece of duct tape off the roll
and slapped it across Gracie's mouth. Her best
weapon, her ability to get people to think from
a different point of view, was silenced.

Regina pushed open the doors to the shed.
Gracie half expected Tyler and Joe to jump
out of the bushes, but the yard was still and
silent. Dark.

There was no movement. She could hear the
low hum of a fishing boat on the bay, trolling
for a good spot, the shushing of the waves
on the sand and the barking of frogs in the
distance. They weren't extremely loud yet,
but before the end of the summer, they would
be.

Her mind was drifting and she forced herself back to the present. She had to be sharp.
Did she hear the quiet whump of a car door
closing? *Please, God, let it be reinforcements.*
She wasn't sure how much longer Marcus had
before he was in serious trouble.

They turned the corner by the pool deck, the
muzzle of Daphne's weapon prodding Gracie
forward.

As they reached the door, Regina pushed
Marcus into a chair on the pool deck and

stepped forward. "What's the code to the lock?"

Gracie raised an eyebrow. Her hands were bound and her mouth taped. She couldn't give them the code.

Regina stepped forward and pulled a knife from one of the pockets of the cargo pants she was wearing. Gracie wondered idly what else she had in those pockets.

The blade gleamed in the moonlight. Regina pressed it against Gracie's ribs. "If you scream, if you so much as make a move that I'm not expecting, you are dead."

Gracie nodded.

Regina ripped the duct tape off her mouth. Gracie swallowed hard but didn't scream. She held her breath as Regina sliced upward through the duct tape around her hands. The knife pierced the fleshy skin at the base of Gracie's thumb. She wanted to cry out, but she couldn't. She breathed, slowly in.

When her hands were free, she walked to the door. Her hands were shaking. It was hard to think beyond the pain from the knife wound, but she had to concentrate. Something was different inside the house.

The light wasn't on in the living room. She knew she'd left it on—she and Tyler had talked about it. Instead, the only light in the house was the tiny light over the stove in the kitchen. And it shone down on a small black flashlight.

Tyler.

Thank you, Jesus.

She had no idea how he'd known, but Tyler and hopefully Joe were waiting in the house for them. She wished she knew what they wanted her to do. The best she could figure is that they wanted her to draw Regina and Daphne into the house.

Her trembling fingers punched the buttons of the code, the gash on her thumb dripping blood. The lock disengaged.

Regina shoved the shotgun into the base of Gracie's spine. Gracie shoved the door and it opened wide. "Regina, the number is in my desk, behind the sofa. We'll have to walk all the way into the room to get to it."

"Daphne, you stay out there with that kid. Keep the gun on him and if anything funky happens, you kill him. Hear me?"

Daphne's eyebrows drew together. "But, I don't kill people."

"You do what I say, Daphne. Think about the money. Think about the house and the pool. Think about all the things she had that you never got."

Gracie shook her head and spoke quietly where only Regina could hear. "You're filling her head with poison. All she needed was a mother who loved her."

"Shut up." Regina's voice was shrill. "Move."

A step and then another. Gracie measured them carefully.

"Hurry up."

She turned to face Regina. "It's dark in here. I don't want you to fall and shoot me by accident."

Gracie took a step away, her heart pounding in her chest. They were close, so close. She could feel it.

Another step brought Regina farther into the house.

The door to the closet and the bedroom slammed open, and Tyler exploded out of the closet, his weapon stretched in front of him. He came out yelling, "Drop the weapon, get your hands in the air, drop the weapon!"

Joe Sheehan stormed the room from the other side, shouting. More shouts came from outside as the CRT simultaneously melted out of the woods and pointed their guns at

Daphne, shouting, like Joe, "Police, you're under arrest, drop the weapon! Get on the ground!"

Regina's eyes went black with rage. She shouted out the door to Daphne, *"Kill him!"*

Joe shoved Regina to the ground and wrestled the shotgun out of her hands. "Got her. Go."

Tyler reached for Gracie's hand and tightly gripped her fingers. "I need to get to Marcus. Are you okay?" he asked hoarsely.

She nodded, blinking back tears. "Thanks to you."

He looked out the door. Daphne still held the gun on Marcus and she looked from Regina on the floor to the CRT, surrounding her.

Gracie pushed Tyler back and took a step toward the door. "You will not put yourself in more danger." His eyes stung as he pulled her close. She allowed herself to relax against him just for a second. He wrapped his other arm around her and pressed a kiss against her hair.

She sighed. Gently, she disentangled herself from Tyler's arms. "It's my job. It's what I do." Two of the members of the Crisis Response Team had blocked the open door with their shields, their automatic weapons held at ready, each aimed solely on Daphne.

Gracie walked to the door and put her hand on one man's back. "Todd, I need to talk to her."

"Not without a vest. Sorry, Doc. Captain's orders." He tapped his earpiece.

With Regina relieved of her weapon and in restraints, Joe stripped his vest off and tossed it to her. "Are you sure you want to do this?"

"I have to do this." She strapped on the bullet-resistant vest and walked back to the door, Tyler right behind her. There was no way he was letting her go out there on her own.

Gracie started to step through the shields and then turned back. "You don't have a vest on, Tyler."

"It's all right, I'm used to it. I need to be there with you and with Marcus. Don't ask me to step aside." His chest ached at the thought of her being in more danger, but he knew that Marcus's best chance of surviving this lay with Gracie's ability to find some kind of common ground with Daphne.

Tyler knew after the other day that it was highly unusual for them to let her negotiate face-to-face. But in this case, she'd been face-to-face with Daphne already. Gracie stepped out the door. The officers shifted so that she could be seen, but they had clearly been told to protect her. One of them handed her an earpiece and she tucked it around her ear.

Daphne held the gun in two hands, pointed at Marcus. He hadn't moved. He needed medical attention. *Now.*

"Daphne, it's Gracie. I know you must be scared. There are a lot of cops here with guns…and they're all very loud and mean-looking."

The two men standing in front of Gracie did look very serious, and they had some serious weaponry. Tyler wouldn't want to cross them. But then again, he also wouldn't want to cross Gracie when she had that determined look on her face.

"It's over. Your mother's been arrested."

Daphne risked a look over her shoulder at Gracie, lines of mascara running down her face. "It isn't over until I say it's over. I started this. I'm going to finish it."

Tyler's palms started to sweat.

"You had everything, Gracie. Everything I should've had." She shifted her hands on the gun, which wobbled but didn't change position.

Gracie's voice was strong and sure. "Everything except a father, Daphne. You got him. All those times I thought he was away on business, he was with the family he considered to be his real family. I was alone here with a nanny. He loved you."

"You don't know that." Daphne pushed blond frizz out of her eyes. "If he loved me, why did he leave everything to you?"

Gracie drew a breath in. "I'm not sure. I've thought about it, though. You had your mother and the house and money that he left to make you comfortable. I didn't have anyone. All I had was the place I lived, the memories I had here."

She took a step closer and pushed the shield aside. Tyler could hear Cruse Conyers yelling in her earpiece from where he stood. Gracie reached up and took it out, letting it dangle over her shoulder.

Tyler went through right behind her, not willing to let her stand in the line of fire alone.

"Daphne, you don't need to be anyone else. Your father loved you because you were you."

Gracie's sister sat down hard on the pool chair beside Marcus. She lowered the gun.

"I didn't want to hurt anyone. I just wanted everything to be okay."

She looked at Tyler, her gray-blue eyes swimming in tears. "I just wanted to make everything be okay again."

He nodded.

Gracie swayed to the side but then planted her feet and managed to stay upright. She had to be exhausted from the adrenaline highs and lows. Tyler put his arm around her, holding her up, as she took another step forward and held out her hand. "Daphne, please, give me the gun. We know you didn't want to hurt anyone. It's time to end this while you still can."

Tears slid down Daphne's face. She turned her hand palm up, with the pistol resting in it. Her face contorted with the kind of emotional pain that came from deep wounds. "I would've been a good sister."

She handed the gun to Gracie.

The CRT erupted in sound and motion as they pulled her away from Gracie and pushed her to the ground.

Tyler turned to Marcus. As gently as he could, he peeled the duct tape off of Marcus's mouth. The kid's eyes popped open. "Is she dead or just under arrest? Did I do good?"

Tyler grabbed his thirteen-year-old brother,

jerking him to his chest and holding him close. "You scared about ten years off of my life, but you did good."

Marcus squirmed out of his grasp. "Okay, seriously. Enough love, dude."

Gracie sat on the other side of Tyler, peeled off the straps of the bullet-resistant vest and tossed it to the ground. She took the knife that Todd from the CRT handed her and sliced through the duct tape holding Marcus's hands together.

Tyler handed Marcus the case with his monitor and the insulin syringes. "Check your blood sugar, shrimp."

For the first time in hours, Tyler could breathe. He turned to Gracie, who looked at him and smiled. And he couldn't take it any more.

He brushed his knuckles down the length of her cheek. It was as soft as he'd imagined it would be. And as she tilted her face into the caress, he leaned forward. He meant to simply brush his lips against hers. A reassurance that they were alive and safe.

But he felt her sweet lips open against his and all thought left his brain. He slid his arm around her ribs and pulled her close, sealing his lips to hers, taking the tender kiss into territory far more delicious and dangerous.

The CRT broke into raucous applause, whistling and stamping. Tyler attempted to pull back, but she didn't let him. Her hands framed his face and she brought his lips back to hers.

And the noise faded away. Until all he could hear was his own heartbeat pounding in his ears.

Her first kiss. Gracie's cheeks heated as she thought of it now, standing at the counter in Tyler's mother's kitchen. Bethanne wasn't letting any of them very far out of her sight.

Gracie hadn't known what to expect from Tyler's mom. After all, it had been Gracie's family that had put Marcus at risk. But there had been no recrimination. Only relief and welcome. Blessing.

She picked a diet soda from the selection on the counter and poured it into a cup.

First kiss *and* second kiss. She hadn't expected it to be so…overwhelming. Actually, she didn't know what she'd expected—toes curling, hair straightening, fireworks exploding. It wasn't that. It was instead a total assault on the senses. One she hadn't wanted to end.

She'd wanted to dive in and experience more.

More feeling, more wonder. Just…more.

His eyes had been on her all night. He hadn't touched her, though when he'd been beside her she'd seen his clenched fist. He'd wanted to.

She licked dry lips and willed the heat in her cheeks to dissipate. Maybe she should open the freezer door and stick her face in it.

"Hi." The deep, gravelly voice at her shoulder made her jump.

"Hi."

"It's getting late. Are you tired?" Tyler's eyes were serious on hers, and there were lines in his face that hadn't been there the day before.

"Exhausted, but wired, too. If that makes any sense."

He nodded. "Do you want to walk outside with me?"

His hand a sweet weight at the small of her back, he guided her to the door. He paused. "Mom, we're going to sit on the porch for a few minutes."

His dad looked up from the newspaper. "Leave the porch light on."

"Funny, Dad."

The feeling in the backyard here was different than the feeling at her home. Instead of open spaces, big pine trees and azalea bushes gave the property a cozy, established feel. It was reassuring, after a day of being exposed in so many ways.

As she relaxed on the outdoor sofa and leaned her head back to look for the stars, she realized Tyler was sitting in a chair studying her.

"Come sit by me. Relax."

"I'm sorry, Gracie." His voice came out a whisper.

"What are you sorry for?"

He paced to the edge of the deck and looked down over the Clarks' yard. "For not protecting you the way I should have, in every way. I shouldn't have kissed you, Gracie. I know you aren't ready for that."

"So you're apologizing for kissing me?" She couldn't help it. She was annoyed.

"No—yes? I'm not sure. I knew what your ground rules were, and I don't want you to think I would ever take advantage of you." The worry on his face melted her resolve to be angry.

She wrapped her hands around his biceps. "We should probably talk about this when we're not tired and wrung out, because when we talk about it, I want to be sure I say exactly what I mean. But this you need to hear now—I don't regret kissing you."

He gave a little half laugh and ran his fingers through his hair. "I don't regret kissing you either."

The porch light flashed off then on again. Tyler sighed. "My dad's way of telling me he's ready for bed. I guess we should go inside before the sheriff comes out."

"Thank you, Tyler."

He looked back from the door. "For what?"

"For being the kind of man who would care whether you crossed a boundary with me tonight." Gracie looked into Tyler's eyes.

She was falling in love with him and falling hard. Trouble was, she had no idea what to do about it.

Monday morning, Gracie sat at her desk with her computer open. She'd been by to check on Daphne this morning. She didn't foresee a time when there would be a relationship between the two of them, but Gracie would make sure that Daphne got the help she needed.

The list of reports to file and the pile of

mail had grown to gargantuan proportions. It threatened to take over Gracie's work space completely if she didn't do something about it. She would do something about it. Later.

The phone rang. "Gracie VanDoren."

"Hey, Doc, it's Cruse Conyers."

"What can I do for you, Cruse?" She picked up an envelope and stuck her finger under the sticky part, ripping it open.

"Do you have any idea why Tyler Clark would call me to ask if he could take you out on a date?"

"Oh." Gracie dropped the letter on her desk. "Wow. I guess Tyler figures you're the closest thing to an authority figure I have, since my dad is gone."

Cruse laughed. "I'm not sure whether to be insulted or complimented by that."

"So what do you think, sir? About Tyler?" She held her breath.

There was silence on the line. Then Cruse said, "I think Tyler is a good guy who went through a rough patch and came out a better man for it. You could do a lot worse."

There was a knock at the half-open door. Tyler. She waved him in.

"Thanks, Cruse. That's what I think, too." She placed the phone on its cradle.

Tyler stood in the door with an enormous bouquet of wildflowers and a vulnerable look in his eyes, one she'd rarely seen from him. "These are for you. Would you like to go to dinner with me?"

Gracie bit her lip, trying not to smile. She looked at her calendar, avoiding his eyes. "Tonight?"

"Every night, Gracie."

She lifted her head to meet his eyes. He was serious.

He didn't smile, not yet. "I know I'm not the guy you were waiting for."

"Oh, Tyler." She crossed to him and placed her hand on his chest, where she could feel the strength of his heartbeat. He closed his eyes. "You are an amazing man with a huge heart, and whatever you decide to do in the future, it's going to be incredible. I'm so proud to know you."

Tyler's lashes were damp when he opened his eyes, his voice husky. He bit his lip, trying to control the trembling as emotion threatened to overwhelm him. "I love you, Gracie. I do. I don't know when it happened or how. And I know I don't deserve you, but you make me believe in good things again."

She stopped his words with her lips on his. "Oh, yes, you do, Tyler Clark. And you were so worth the wait."

EPILOGUE

"You ready?" Tyler looked at Gracie, his heart in his throat, about to take the final step in the find-a-life plan.

"Am I ready?" His wife laughed. "This is the easy part. Quitting my job, that was hard."

"Like you really quit. Conyers calls you every other day for expert consultation."

She held her face up for a kiss, her big blue eyes sparkling. "Haven't you learned that I'm indispensible?"

"Baby, you were indispensible from the first minute I met you." He wrapped his arms around her and swung her around, her silky skirt swirling with her. These days, she was more prone to wearing flip-flops than high heels. Running back and forth between her new home office and the upper floors to answer questions for the construction crew was too much with heels on, even for her.

Her arms came up around his neck and he got that feeling in his chest. Happiness? Yeah, that was it. He leaned toward her. "I love you."

She went still, her boundless energy on pause for a second. "I love you, too. You've brought my lonely life lots of joy, Tyler Clark."

"Same goes, Gracie Clark." He asked her again. "You ready?"

"There's about a hundred people out there around the pool waiting for us to make the announcement. I guess we should go."

He agreed. "No turning back now."

"Do you want to?" She asked, suddenly serious.

Tyler shook his head. "No. It's right."

"Yeah, it is. We were meant to do this together." She held out her hand and he grasped it with his larger, sturdier hand and opened the door.

Gracie stood behind the podium, her palms going sweaty as she looked into the cameras. They'd invited the press because they wanted the word to get out—into the right people's hands, the people who needed it.

"Good afternoon. Welcome to Restoration

Cove." She surreptitiously wiped her hands on her skirt and placed them on the podium. Matt's mom and dad smiled at her from the front of the crowd. "Tyler and I have invited you here for the grand opening of our B&B because you are all, in some way, special to us."

She looked around at the group assembled. These weren't just friends. Her captain, Cruse Conyers, had given her away at her wedding. The members of the Crisis Response Team were in many ways her brothers. Maria Storm and her husband, Ben. They were family, too.

She, who had thought she was all alone after her mom and dad died, was blessed with a huge, loving family who had helped her through her crisis. And that support system is what she and Tyler wanted to give other people.

"So many of you helped me last spring when I was in a tough spot. And I know, if any one of us were in need, we would be there for each other." She looked at Tyler. "That's what family is for."

He put his arm around her, his warm fingers sliding to curve around her ribs. He leaned forward to the microphone. "Not everyone is as blessed as we are. Not everyone has family to turn to in times of crisis. Many law enforcement officers and agents feel isolated and alone after traumatic events. Restoration Cove is here for them, offering a stay here at the B&B, on a sliding payscale, for as long as they need it.

"We'll offer a full range of therapeutic services for those who need it. And for those who don't, we offer a relaxing vacation away from the stressors of life."

Gracie stepped to the side, where a small table had been set up with a laptop. Tyler handed her the microphone. "As of right now, the website is live. We are open for business and taking reservations."

At that exact moment, Tyler's cell phone rang. The crowd erupted in applause.

"We're happy to answer any questions that you may have." She placed the microphone back in the stand.

Cruse Conyers shouted out, "Who's going to be doing the cooking?"

Gracie leaned forward. "Tyler is supervising the kitchen."

"Thank goodness," Todd from the CRT shouted.

"Very funny, guys. Any more questions?"

* * *

Three hours later, Gracie found Tyler in the now renovated pool house that they shared, his laptop open, a concerned look on his face. Her cat was curled up on the couch beside him. She sat down and put her hand on his arm. "It's okay, babe. The reservations will come. It's only the first day."

"That's not the problem." Exhaling slowly, he turned to face her. "We're already booked through Easter."

Tyler closed the laptop and placed it on the coffee table. He put his arm around his wife and pulled her onto his lap. Charlemagne complained loudly about being displaced and jumped down, his tail twitching as he sauntered to his place under the desk.

She sighed. "Long, *long* day."

"Yeah, but we're home now." He let his voice go low and deep and placed a kiss at that spot where her neck met her shoulder. The one that always made her shiver. Catching her breath, she gave him that look. The one from under her eyelashes.

He stood, swinging her up into his arms and started toward the bedroom they shared. "Oh yeah, you were so worth the wait."

* * * * *

Dear Reader,

Sometimes when change happens it feels like the ground is unsteady. Changing and adapting to a new reality isn't easy.

Gracie and Tyler had their own journey to peace in the midst of change. Tyler's life took an unexpected turn when he had to leave the DEA. After living other people's lives as an undercover agent, he had to learn to trust people with his true persona and trust God with the new plan for his own life. Gracie discovered that while the things that she believed to be true about her family weren't, God hadn't changed. He was still, and would forever be, the same God she knew. He is always trustworthy.

I feel sure that your life journey, like mine, is filled with hairpin turns and unexpected drops, the occasional valley and many a mountain to climb. My prayer for you is that you know that when everything else changes, the God of the universe remains the same.

Thanks so much for reading *Point Blank Protector*. I'd love to hear from you! To contact me, or for more information and updates on the Emerald Coast 911 series, visit my Web site at www.stephanienewtonbooks.com.

Many blessings,

Stephanie Newton

QUESTIONS FOR DISCUSSION

1. When Tyler meets Gracie, he doesn't have the best attitude. What changes his mind?

2. Gracie tells Tyler that she doesn't date. What is Tyler's first response?

3. How is Tyler's outlook on Gracie's decision not to date different from that of other men Gracie knows?

4. Tyler had to completely reinvent himself. What were some of the things he did in his find-a-life plan? Why?

5. What was Gracie's response when she found out about her father's secret life?

6. Tyler has three brothers. How do you think this influenced him growing up? How do they influence him now?

7. Every aspect of Gracie's life felt like it had been invaded. How did Gracie handle the pressure?

8. Daphne believed that she should have everything in her life that Gracie had been given. Have you ever justified your actions according to what you believed you deserved?

9. Gracie held Shay Smith accountable for her actions, something Shay eventually thanked her for. Why do you think we sometimes have to face hard truths before we can truly change?

10. Families are complicated. Do you think your family affects what you think about yourself?

11. Do you think that Gracie will be able to trust Tyler after finding out that her father kept so many secrets?

12. Tyler and Gracie chose a different path for their life than the one they thought they were going to be traveling. What did they choose to do with the property that Gracie inherited?

13. Have you ever had to choose a different

path for yourself? What influenced your decision? Was it more difficult or easier than you thought it would be? Why?

LARGER-PRINT BOOKS!

GET 2 FREE
LARGER-PRINT NOVELS
PLUS 2 FREE
MYSTERY GIFTS

Love Inspired

SUSPENSE
RIVETING INSPIRATIONAL ROMANCE

Larger-print novels are now available...

LARGER-PRINT BOOKS!

GET 2 FREE
LARGER-PRINT NOVELS
PLUS 2 FREE
MYSTERY GIFTS

Love Inspired

Larger-print novels are now available...

LILP11